# CAPTIVE OF FRIENDLY COVE

### Based on the Secret Journals of John Jewitt

by Rebecca Goldfield
and Mike Short
with Matt Dembicki
and Evan Keeling

Rebecca Goldfield, writer

Mike Short, penciler

Matt Dembicki, inker

Evan Keeling, colorist

Library of Congress Cataloging-in-Publication Data

Goldfield, Rebecca, 1953-
  Captive of Friendly Cove : based on the secret journals of John Jewitt / text by Rebecca Goldfield; illustrations by Mike Short.
    pages cm
  ISBN 978-1-936218-11-0 (paperback)
1.  Jewitt, John Rodgers, 1783-1821--Juvenile literature. 2.  Jewitt, John Rodgers, 1783-1821--Comic books, strips, etc. 3.  Nootka Indians--Juvenile literature. 4.  Nootka Indians--Comic books, strips, etc. 5.  Indian captivities--British Columbia--Juvenile literature. 6.  Indian captivities--British Columbia--Comic books, strips, etc. 7.  Nootka Sound (B.C.)--History--Juvenile literature. 8.  Nootka Sound (B.C.)--History--Comic books, strips, etc. 9.  Graphic novels. I. Short, Mike (Michael Theodore), 1973- II. Title.
  E99.N85G65 2015
  971.1004'97955--dc23

                                2015016833

Printed in the United States
0  9  8  7  6  5  4  3  2  1

Fulcrum Publishing
4690 Table Mountain Dr., Ste. 100
Golden, CO 80403
800-992-2908 • 303-277-1623
www.fulcrumbooks.com

With love to the two Berts—Rob and Al—
and in memory of the singular Bina

RG


To Danette, Colin, and Marcus

MS

# From the Author

I first encountered John Rodgers Jewitt in Horseshoe Bay, British Columbia, when I stumbled upon a curious shop—a mix of an ice-cream parlor, post office, and bookstore. A few minutes later, I was eating a maple ice-cream cone while poking through books on a creaky rotating rack. One book in particular caught my eye: *White Slaves of Maquinna*. It told the story of John Jewitt, a nineteen-year-old British armorer and blacksmith who was fascinated by the writings of navigators such as James Cook and by stories of the New World from sailors he'd often meet while growing up in the port city of Hull, England.

John got his chance to embark on his own adventure in 1802 when an American trading ship, the *Boston*, arrived in Hull. The ship needed repairs and provisions for a voyage to the Pacific Northwest of the Americas. John was thrilled when her captain invited him along on the next voyage, and he left his friends and family with absolutely no idea of the disaster the ship would soon meet.

I read the whole book in one day. "What a great story for a graphic novel!" I thought when I'd finished. Because the story took place long before the camera age, I first had to consider what things might have looked like back then, and how this would translate to a graphic novel. Luckily for me, famous navigator James Cook had the artist John Webber with him on his voyage. Spanish sea captains also had artists aboard—people such as José Cardero, José Maria Vasquez, and Manuel Garsia. I studied all these images closely and then explored museums to see the clothing, weaponry, masks, and indigenous art from this time period. I read every book I could find about the story.

Most exciting of all, I finally made my way to Nootka Island on a converted minesweeper boat, docking at Yuquot (which John would have known as Friendly Cove). There, I spent a perfect summer day as a guest of the Nuu-chah-nulth people, who had invited the public to experience their culture and to feast on barbecued salmon. Several Mowachaht people shared with me information about their culture and their interpretation of John's story. I combined all I learned from as many sources as possible, but mostly stayed close to John's point of view. In the end, I also relied upon my imagination as to what life there might have looked and felt like back then. Adding my ideas and words to his, I tried to keep the spirit of John alive.

And that's one of the great joys of writing a book such as this. You get to bring a person back to life. Comics are justly famous for their superheroes, but in our book you will meet a peaceful young man who stumbled into a turbulent and conflict-filled world; struggled for survival; faced hunger, cold, fear, and loneliness; and ultimately helped break a long cycle of bloodshed. For that, he is a hero, too.

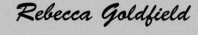

# Foreword

The adventures of John Jewitt have fascinated readers for more than 200 years. The story is an actual historical event that took place in the first decade of the 1800s in Nootka Sound, located on the west coast of Vancouver Island, British Columbia, Canada. Jewitt kept a journal of his 851 days as a slave of a Mowachaht (Nootka) chief, which he published in 1807. A much longer narrative was published in 1815, with an additional theatrical presentation enjoying a brief run in Philadelphia in 1817. This latest publication, presented here in a graphic novel format, is the first of its kind—a truly unique presentation of Jewitt's remarkable story.

The setting for this epic tale of survival, Nootka Sound, is the territory of the Mowachaht, "people of the deer," whose head chief still carries the name Maquinna to this day. Yuquot, meaning "where the wind blows from all directions," was the main village of the Mowachaht until 1966, when they moved farther inland on Vancouver Island. To the early European and American visitors, the area was known as Friendly Cove.

In the late eighteenth century, the North Pacific was an unknown region to the Western world, yet a focal point of international politics between the two great European maritime powers: Spain and Britain. Both countries sent several expeditions to chart the coastline, each vying for European control over the region. The Spanish even maintained a military garrison at Nootka Sound from 1789 to 1795. Cook, Bodega y Quadra, Vancouver, and Malaspina—all famous sea captains of the era—spent time in Nootka Sound. As knowledge spread that sea otter pelts, abundant in the North Pacific, brought high prices in China, Nootka Sound became an economic center of the fur trade on the Northwest Coast. Nootka Sound was a favorite port of call with more than 100 trading vessels visiting between 1785 and 1795.

But the coming together of the European and American traders with the indigenous peoples of the Northwest Coast often led to misunderstandings and, at times, violence. John Jewitt, a young British blacksmith and armorer, experienced that violence firsthand in 1803, when he arrived in Friendly Cove as part of the crew of an American ship, the *Boston*.

Today, the west coast of Vancouver Island is largely a wilderness, with only occasional First Nation communities as reminders of the rich historical past. One native family still resides at the Mowachaht village of Yuquot. This great adventure story lives on while inspiring a new kind of telling—a graphic novel.

*Richard Inglis*

Richard Inglis, former head of anthropology at the Royal British Columbia Museum, has written extensively about the contact and maritime fur trade period of the Pacific Northwest. He works closely with the Mowachaht-Muchalaht First Nations on heritage and cultural projects.

# Contents

On September 3, 1802, a young
English blacksmith named John Jewitt
boarded the trading ship *Boston*,
eager to begin a new life in the New World.

For years, he'd heard sailors
describing their adventures
in the "Indian trade"...

... but nothing could have ever prepared
him for the ordeal he would experience
when he arrived off the west coast
of Vancouver Island, six months later.

His journals survive to tell the tale
of what happened when the ship's
captain clashed with a proud Nootkan chief.

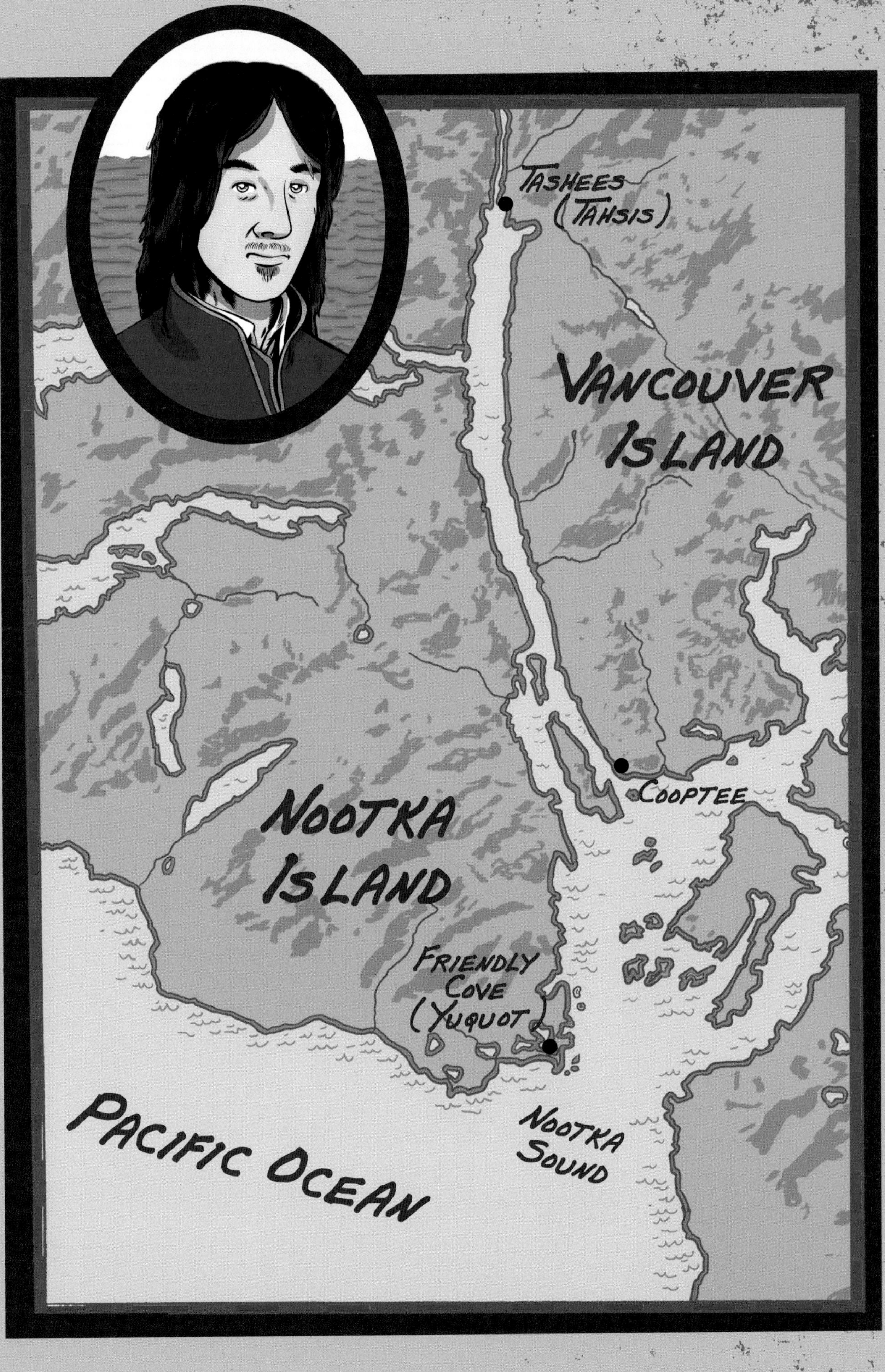
TASHEES
(TAHSIS)
VANCOUVER
ISLAND
COOPTEE
NOOTKA
ISLAND
FRIENDLY
COVE
(YUQUOT)
PACIFIC OCEAN
NOOTKA
SOUND

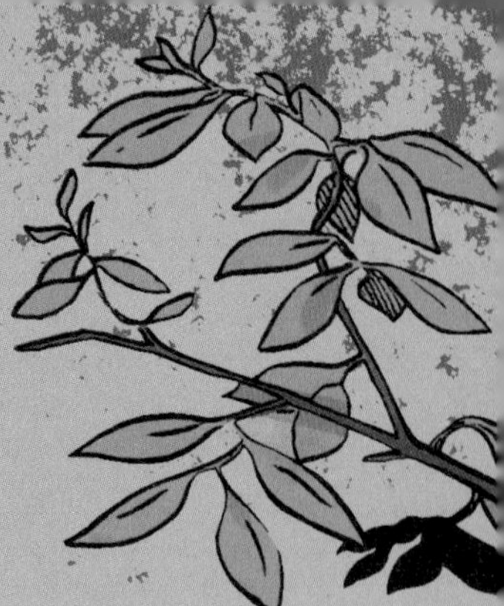

# CHAPTER 1
## Friendly Cove

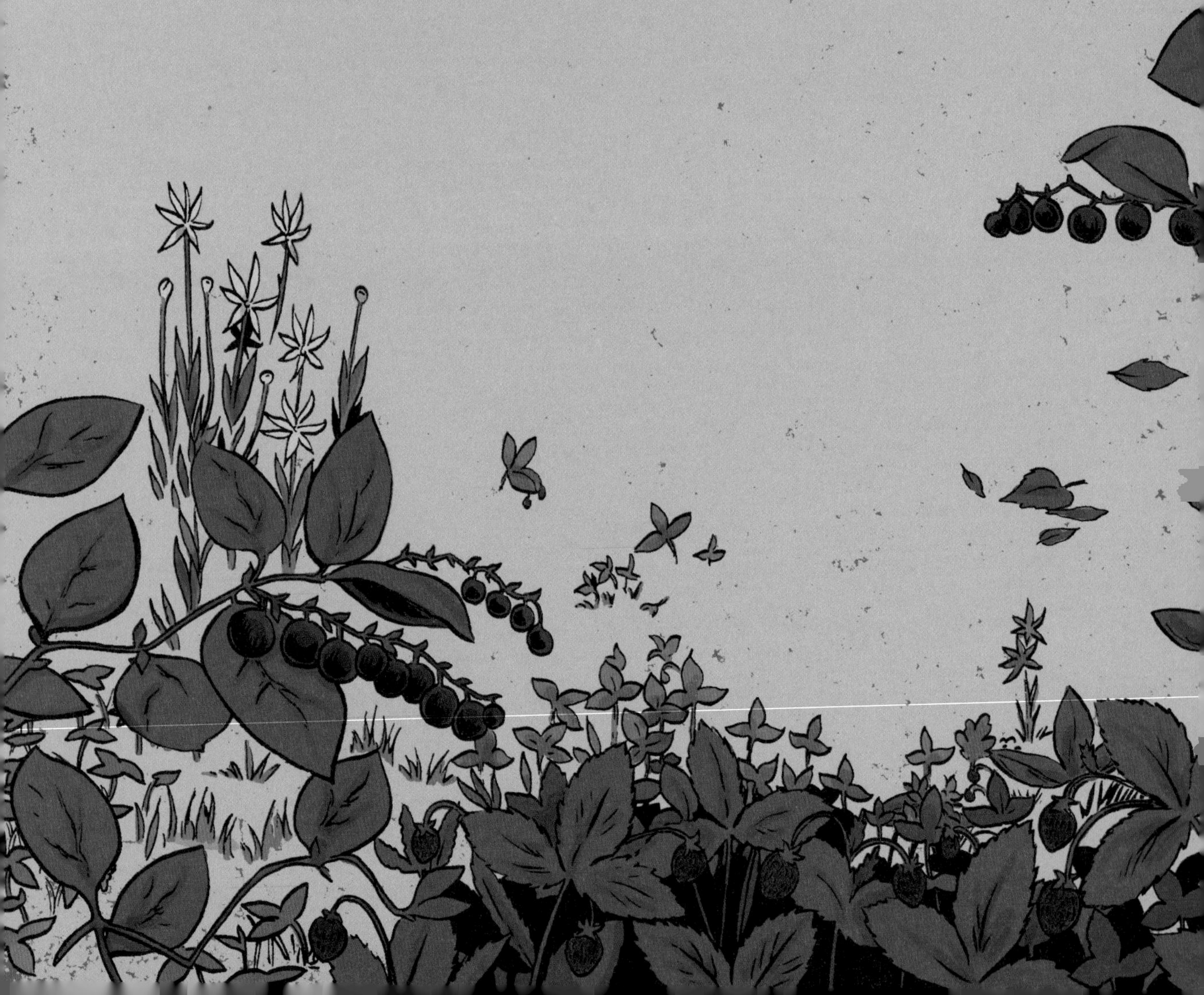

MARCH 12, 1803
MY SHIP FINALLY ARRIVED IN NOOTKA SOUND, THE MEN PARCHED WITH THIRST AND THE BOSTON BATTERED BY THE OCEAN STORMS WE HAD ENDURED. WE DROPPED ANCHOR NEAR A NATIVE VILLAGE CALLED FRIENDLY COVE, SEEKING WATER TO DRINK AND TIMBER TO REPAIR OUR SHIP.

OUR CAPTAIN, JOHN SALTER, DESIRED ONLY A BRIEF STAY.

MY MATES, MOSTLY AMERICAN, DESIRED PERHAPS A BIT MORE TIME...

AS FOR ME, I WAS TOO BUSY FORGING WEAPONS FOR THE INDIAN TRADE TO THINK OF ANYTHING ELSE.

I HAD ALWAYS DREAMED OF SEEING THIS BEAUTIFUL LAND, BUT THERE WAS WORD THAT THE TRIBES TO THE NORTH WERE FEROCIOUS.

NOW, I COULD ONLY PRAY THAT THE VILLAGE OF FRIENDLY COVE WOULD LIVE UP TO ITS NAME.

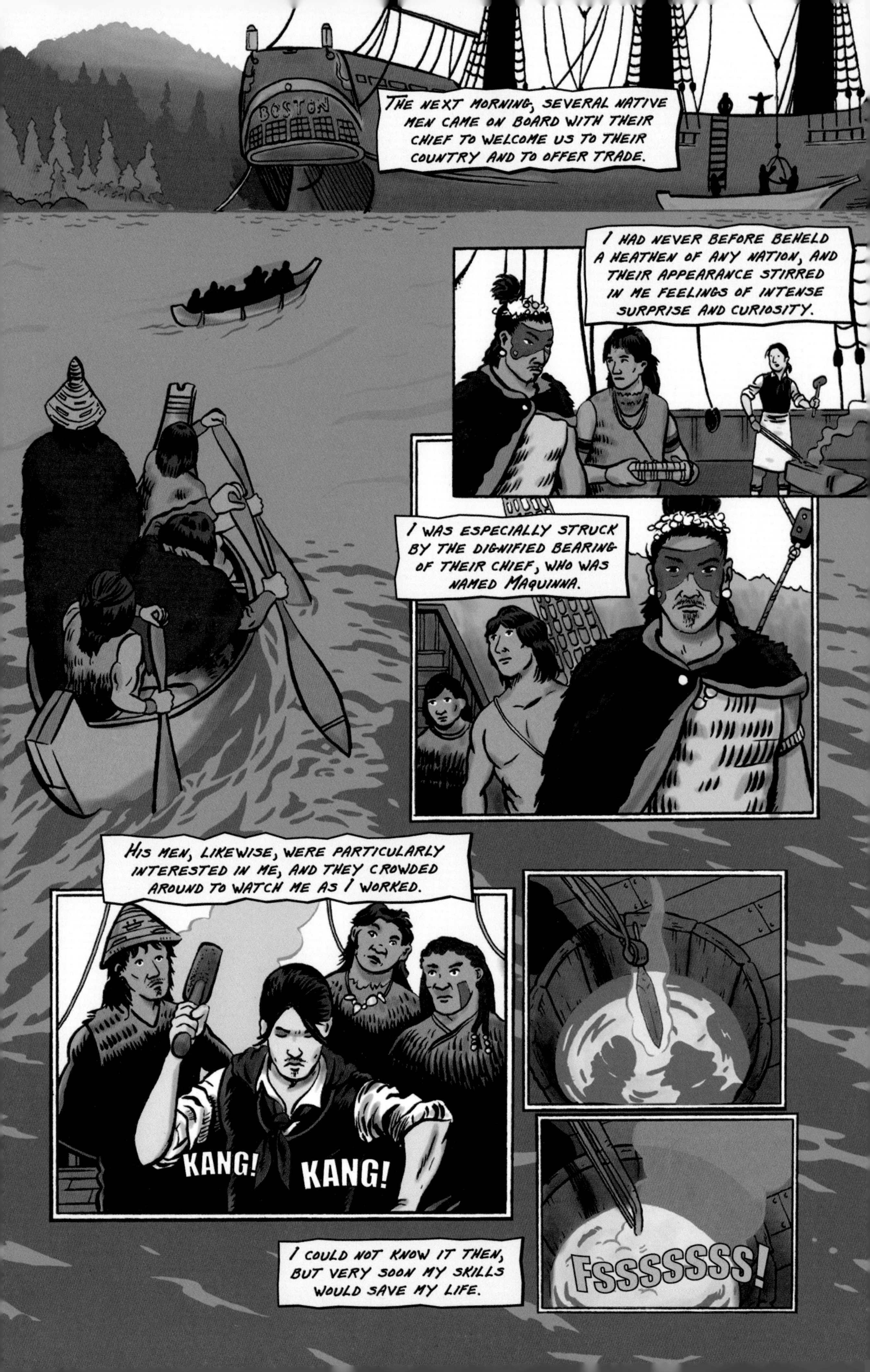
BOSTON
THE NEXT MORNING, SEVERAL NATIVE MEN CAME ON BOARD WITH THEIR CHIEF TO WELCOME US TO THEIR COUNTRY AND TO OFFER TRADE.
I HAD NEVER BEFORE BEHELD A HEATHEN OF ANY NATION, AND THEIR APPEARANCE STIRRED IN ME FEELINGS OF INTENSE SURPRISE AND CURIOSITY.
I WAS ESPECIALLY STRUCK BY THE DIGNIFIED BEARING OF THEIR CHIEF, WHO WAS NAMED MAQUINNA.
HIS MEN, LIKEWISE, WERE PARTICULARLY INTERESTED IN ME, AND THEY CROWDED AROUND TO WATCH ME AS I WORKED.
KANG!
KANG!
FSSSSSSS!
I COULD NOT KNOW IT THEN, BUT VERY SOON MY SKILLS WOULD SAVE MY LIFE.

I DON'T TRUST THEM. THEY CAN BE THIEVISH.

ON MARCH 19, A NUMBER OF NATIVES CAME ON BOARD BEARING GREAT QUANTITIES OF FRESH SALMON.

I DON'T TRUST THEM. THEY CAN BE VIOLENT.

WE WELCOME YOU, SIR.

TO SHOW HIS GOODWILL, CAPTAIN SALTER SOON INVITED MAQUINNA AND HIS CHIEFS TO DINE WITH HIM.

THEY DID NOT CARE FOR THE TASTE OF SALT, BUT WERE FOND OF OUR BREAD DIPPED IN MOLASSES.

WE HAVE MUCH WILD DUCK AND GOOSE HERE.

EXCELLENT NEWS INDEED!

PLEASE ACCEPT THIS GIFT OF A WEAPON FOR THE HUNT.

WITH GIFTS NOW HAVING BEEN EXCHANGED, I EXPECTED OUR SHORT STAY TO PROCEED WELL.

WE WILL BRING MANY BIRDS FOR YOUR MEN TO EAT.

BY MARCH 21, WE HAD TAKEN ON WHAT WOOD AND WATER WE REQUIRED, AND PREPARED FOR DEPARTURE TO THE NORTH.

THERE, WE HOPED TO OBTAIN SEA OTTER PELTS FOR TRADE IN CHINA.

LATER THAT DAY, MAQUINNA CAME ON BOARD WITH NINE PAIR OF GEESE AS A PRESENT.

PESHAK.

BUT ON THIS VISIT HE SEEMED MUCH TROUBLED.

PESHAK. BAD. THE GUN IS BAD. PESHAK.

HMMM...

HE BROKE IT HIMSELF!

WHAP!

YOU, SIR, INSULT MY GIFT AND ME!

THE CAPTAIN CALLED MAQUINNA A LIAR AND MANY OTHER OFFENSIVE THINGS. AND THE CHIEF UNDERSTOOD EVERY WORD.

THE CHIEF STRUGGLED TO SUPPRESS HIS FURY.

9

MAQUINNA SAID NOT A WORD IN REPLY.

BUT I WATCHED HIM REPEATEDLY PUT HIS HAND TO HIS THROAT...

...AND THEN RUB HIS CHEST.

I LITTLE UNDERSTOOD THIS GESTURE, BUT HIS RAGE WAS CLEAR.

I LATER LEARNED THAT IT WAS TO KEEP DOWN HIS HEART, WHICH MAQUINNA FELT RISING UP INTO HIS THROAT.

HE SOON RETURNED TO SHORE WITH HIS MEN, EVIDENTLY MUCH DISTURBED.

I WAS CERTAIN THEY WOULD NOT OVERLOOK THE INSULT.

THE FOLLOWING MORNING, MAQUINNA'S MEN AGAIN BROUGHT SALMON TO US, AS AMERICAN CAPTAINS ARE MORE WILLING TO ALLOW NATIVES ON BOARD THAN WE BRITISH ARE.

ONE OF THEM APPEARED WEARING A STRANGE WOODEN MASK.

GOOD MORNING, CAPTAIN!

MAQUINNA SEEMED IN A REMARKABLY GOOD MOOD.

IT IS YOUR FRIEND, THE CHIEF!

HIS PEOPLE SANG AND CAPERED AROUND THE DECK TO ENTERTAIN US, WHILE MAQUINNA USED A WHISTLE TO DIRECT THEIR MOTIONS.

WELL DONE! MOST ENJOYABLE!

IT WAS AS THOUGH THE RECENT QUARREL HAD BEEN FORGOTTEN.

CAPTAIN, WHEN DO YOU PLAN TO GO BACK TO SEA?

TOMORROW.

YOU LOVE SALMON. THERE IS MUCH IN FRIENDLY COVE. WHY NOT GO AND CATCH SOME?

MAQUINNA AND HIS CHIEFS STAYED AND DINED ON BOARD.

LATER, TEN OF OUR MEN WENT TO FISH AT FRIENDLY COVE. THUS WERE OUR NUMBERS DIVIDED.

I DESCENDED TO MY WORKBENCH TO CONTINUE CLEANING MUSKETS.

ABOUT AN HOUR LATER, I HEARD A GREAT BUSTLE AND CONFUSION ON DECK.

THUMP!

WHUMP!

CRASH!

ALL AT ONCE, I WAS YANKED BY MY HAIR, WHICH I WORE SHORT.

FORTUNATELY FOR ME, THE RIBBON SLIPPED...

...AND SO I ESCAPED THE FULL FORCE OF A BLOW THAT OTHERWISE WOULD HAVE SPLIT MY HEAD IN TWO!

LEAVE THE ARMORER ALONE.

I MAY HAVE USE FOR HIM.

I LAY STUNNED AND SENSELESS. HOW LONG I CONTINUED IN THIS CONDITION I KNOW NOT.

As I slowly recovered my senses below deck, the shouts and yells from above told me my mates were being slaughtered.

It was as though I were in a hideous dream... from which I could not awaken.

CRACK!

NEVER SHALL I FORGET MY IMPRESSION OF THOSE DREADFUL MOMENTS.

AT EVERY TURN, I EXPECTED TO SHARE THE FATE OF MY UNFORTUNATE COMPANIONS.

AND WHEN I HEARD THE SONGS OF TRIUMPH, WHICH FOLLOWED THE TERRIBLE YELLS, THE BLOOD RAN COLD IN MY VEINS.

I THOUGHT THEY HAD SPARED ME ONLY TO TORTURE AND KILL ME LATER. I REMAINED IN THIS HORRID STATE OF SUSPENSE FOR A VERY LONG TIME.

THEN MAQUINNA, CALLING ME BY NAME, ORDERED ME TO COME UP.

MARCH 22, 1803, MARKED MY LAST DAY AS A FREE MAN.

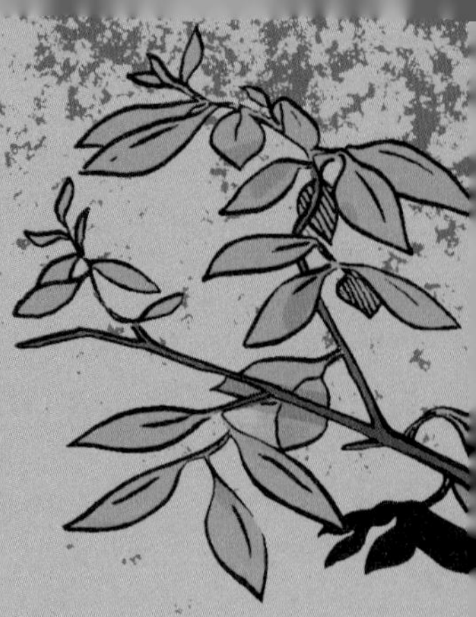

# CHAPTER 2
## Deadly Cove

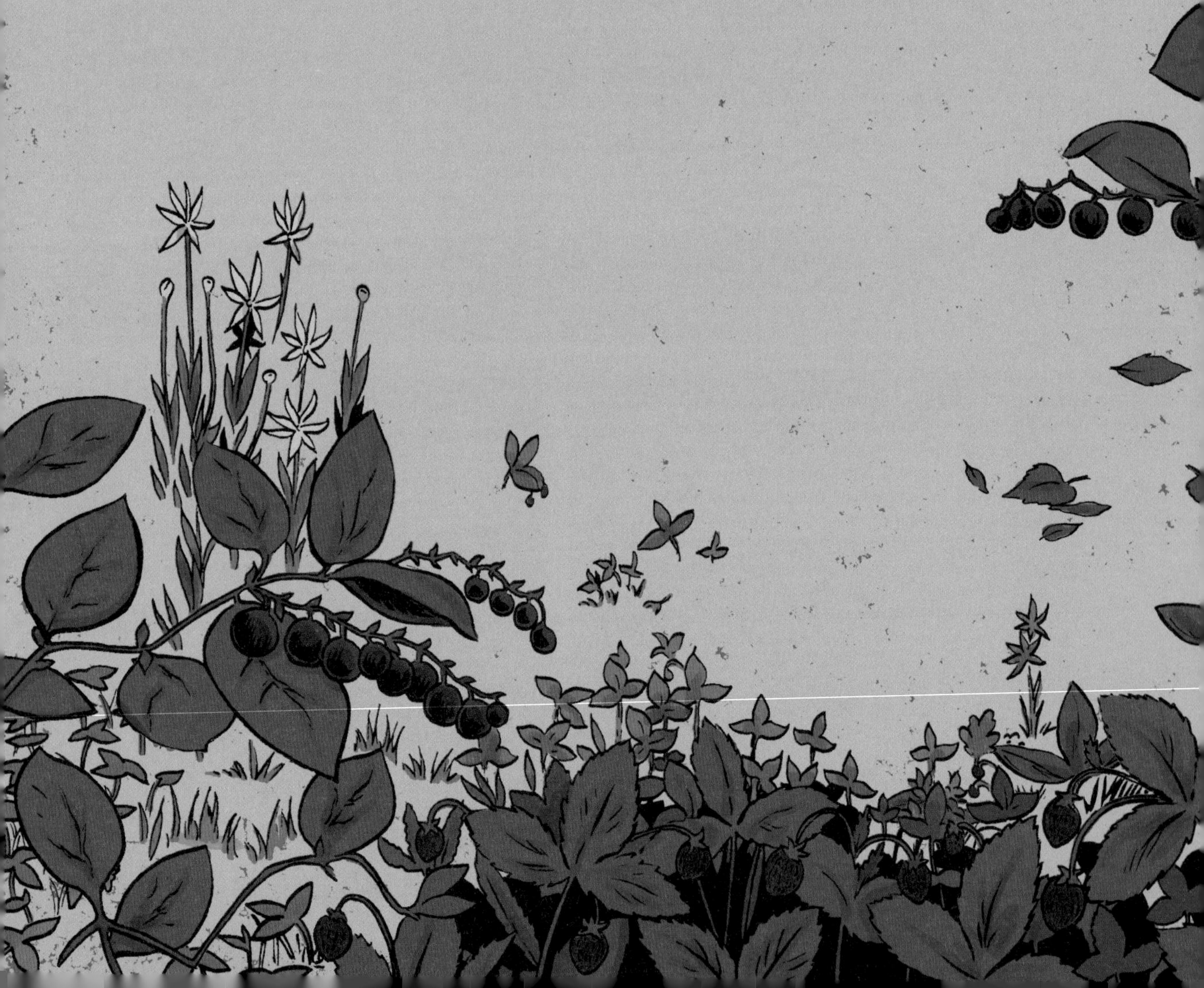

I GROPED MY WAY UP AS BEST AS I COULD...

...BLINDED BY MY OWN BLOOD.

CLEAN HIM UP!

SPLOOSH!

I COULD STILL SEE CLEARLY FROM ONE OF MY EYES. AND WHAT A TERRIBLE SPECTACLE IT WAS!

SIX WARRIORS COVERED IN MY COMRADES' BLOOD, PREPARED TO STRIKE AGAIN.

I THOUGHT MY LAST MOMENT HAD COME... AND PREPARED MY SOUL TO MEET MY MAKER!

I SPEAK. YOU NO SAY NO.

YOU SAY NO—DAGGER COME!

BE MY SLAVE. OR DIE NOW!

YOU WILL MAKE MY DAGGERS. REPAIR MY MUSKETS. FIGHT IN MY BATTLES.

MAQUINNA OFFERED TO SPARE MY LIFE IF I AGREED...

...AND ORDERED ME TO SHOW MY SUBMISSION.

BUT HE WAS ALONE IN SHOWING ME MERCY.

KILL HIM!

KILL HIM!

KILL HIM!

KILL HIM!

I SAY MY SLAVE SHALL LIVE!

DRINK THIS NOW. YOU WILL NEED IT.

THEN MAQUINNA LED ME TO THE MOST GRUESOME SIGHT I HAD EVER SEEN.

BEFORE ME LAY THE HEADS OF THE *BOSTON* CREW... ALL TWENTY-FIVE OF THEM.

WHO IS THIS?

EDWARD THOMPSON. THE BOATSWAIN.

ABRAHAM WATERS. THE STEWARD.

JOHN WILSON. THE COOK.

AND HIM?

MY CAPTAIN.

THE ENTIRE CREW
HAD BEEN MASSACRED.

I CANNOT DESCRIBE WHAT
I FELT AT THAT MOMENT.
BUT THERE WAS NO TIME
TO ABSORB THE SHOCK
OF IT ALL.

THE CHIEF QUICKLY DRESSED MY
WOUNDS AND ISSUED HIS FIRST
COMMAND TO ME, HIS NEW SLAVE.

MAKE
FOR FRIENDLY
COVE!

BUT I KNEW NOW
THERE WOULD BE NOTHING
FRIENDLY FOR ME THERE.

SEVERAL HOURS LATER, WITH THE ADVANTAGE OF A FAIR WIND, I SUCCEEDED IN GETTING THE SHIP INTO THE COVE.

Crruuunch!

BY ORDER OF THE CHIEF, I RAN THE BOSTON AGROUND.

WE WERE RECEIVED BY THE INHABITANTS OF THE VILLAGE WITH LOUD SHOUTS OF JOY...

WOCASH TYEE!**

WOCASH!*

*GOOD **GOOD KING

...AND THE HORRIBLE SOUND OF DRUMMING WITH STICKS UPON THE ROOFS AND SIDES OF THEIR HOUSES. THUS THEY WELCOMED THEIR CHIEF HOME.

I WAS TAKEN TO THE LARGEST HOUSE IN THE VILLAGE.

It was Maquinna's home. Among the people within were many women.

Several of them seemed to be his wives.

They murmured words of sympathy in soothing tones and gently patted my head.

DO NOT FEAR US.

WE WILL CARE FOR YOU.

But I found no such kindness from the men!

I CUT THE SAILORS' THROATS WITH THEIR OWN KNIVES!

WE SHOULD CUT THIS MAMETHLEE'S* THROAT, TOO.

*A NAME FOR A PERSON OF EUROPEAN DESCENT

THE MEN WERE MUCH DISSATISFIED THAT I HAD BEEN ALLOWED TO LIVE, AND URGED MAQUINNA TO PUT ME TO DEATH.

DO NOT TOUCH MY SLAVE!

I HAVE PROMISED HIM HIS LIFE, AND I HAVE DECIDED HE WILL MAKE ARMS FOR ME.

MAQUINNA THEN HAD HIS WOMEN BRING FOOD.

EAT! EAT MUCH! IT WILL MAKE YOU STRONG.

BUT TO ME, THEIR OFFERINGS WERE LOATHSOME.

IT WAS THEN THAT A YOUNG BOY APPROACHED ME.

I AM SAT-SAT-SOK-SIS, THE SON OF TYEE MAQUINNA.

THE PRINCE WAS AN AFFECTIONATE CHILD.

I AM CALLED JOHN.

CWAN...

AND I SAW A CHANCE TO GAIN THE GOODWILL OF HIS FATHER.

I CUT THE BUTTONS OFF MY COAT TO FASHION AN ORNAMENT FOR THE BOY, WHICH DELIGHTED HIM.

MAQUINNA, TOO, WAS PLEASED BY THIS.

YOU SLEEP, NEXT TO MY SON.

YOUR ENEMIES WILL NOT DARE COME CLOSE TO HIM.

BUT I COULD FIND NO REST, FOR THE PAIN IN MY HEAD AND THE FEAR IN MY STOMACH KEPT ME AWAKE.

NEAR MIDNIGHT, TO MY GREAT ALARM, ONE OF THE MEN APPEARED.

THERE IS NEWS.

WE HAVE FOUND ANOTHER MAMETHLEE IN THE SHIP.

ALIVE!

WHEN THE SUN RISES, I WILL KILL HIM MYSELF.

I BEG OF YOU, SIR, DO NOT HARM THE SAILOR.

SILENCE, SLAVE.

I THOUGHT THE SURVIVOR MIGHT BE *John Thompson,* A SAILMAKER.

HE HAD BEEN WORKING BELOW JUST BEFORE THE ATTACK, AND I HAD NOT SEEN HIS REMAINS AMONGST THOSE UNFORTUNATE OTHERS.

WHAT COMFORT, WHAT CONSOLATION IT WOULD BE TO HAVE A FELLOW COUNTRYMAN FOR A COMPANION, ONE WHO MIGHT LIGHTEN THE BURDEN OF MY SLAVERY.

I LAY AWAKE ALL THAT FIRST NIGHT IN *Friendly Cove,* DESPERATE TO DEVISE A PLAN TO SAVE HIS LIFE... WHOEVER HE MIGHT BE!

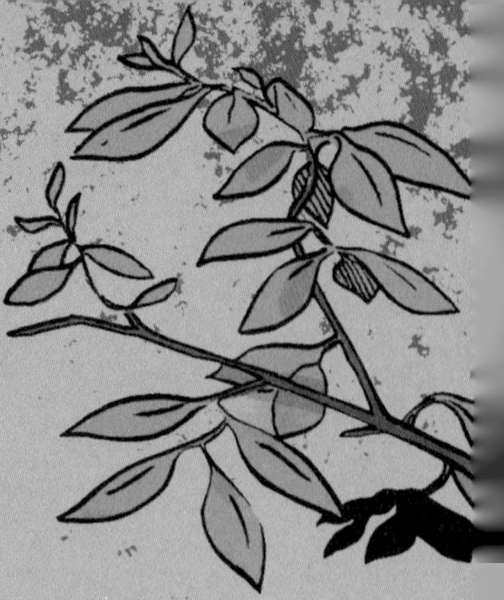

# CHAPTER 3
## The Lie

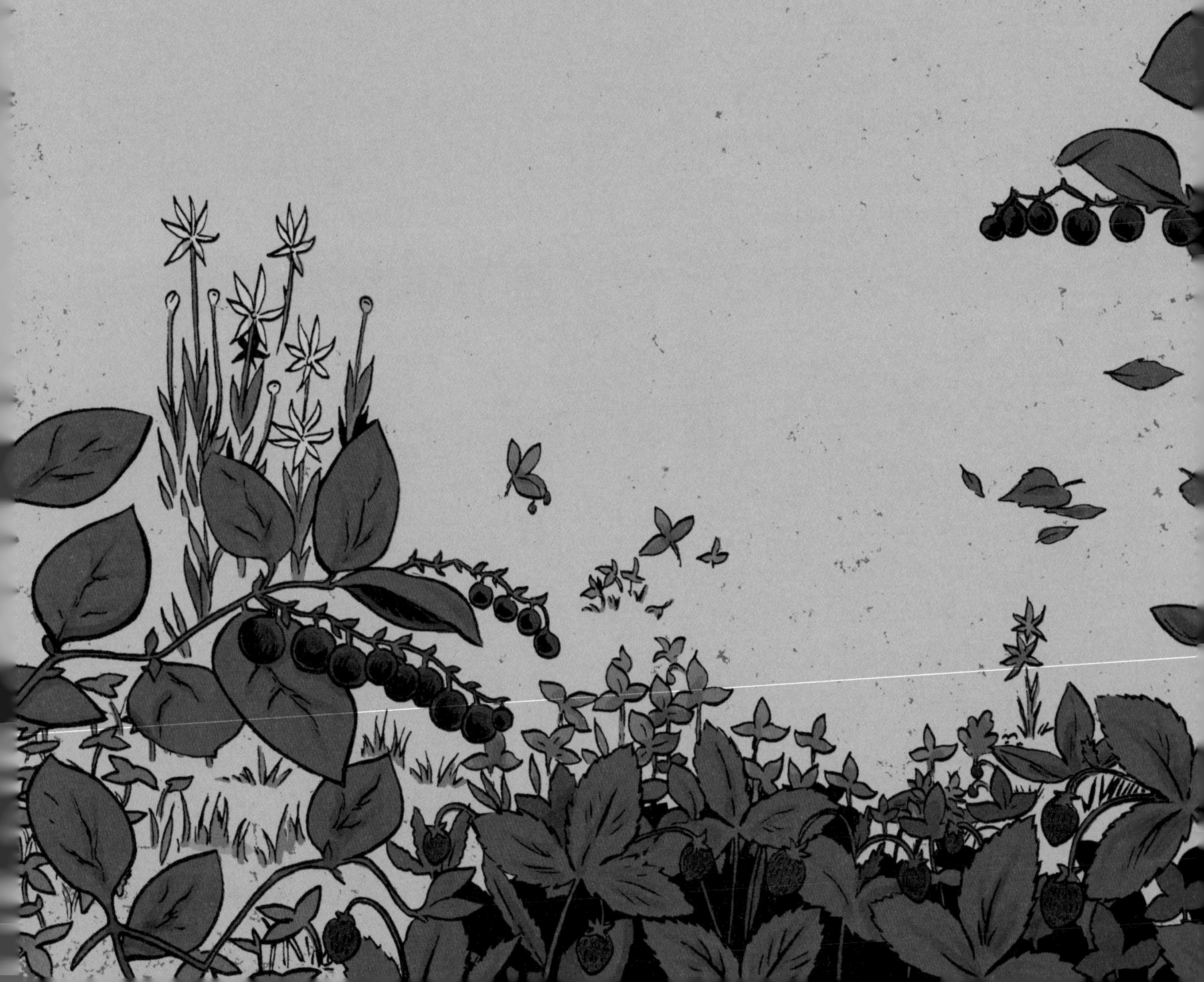

THE QUESTION OF MY FELLOW SAILOR'S FATE WAS TAKEN UP AT DAWN.

YOU— FOLLOW ME.

I STILL DID NOT KNOW WHO HAD SURVIVED THE MASSACRE.

ANOTHER MAMETHLEE HAS BEEN FOUND, STILL ON THE SHIP.

I ASK OP YOU: DOES HE LIVE OR DIE?

I KNEW I HAD PRECIOUS LITTLE TIME TO ACT.

HE DIES!

HE DIES!

HE DIES!

HE DIES!

HE DIES!

MY CHIEF, YOUR SLAVE ASKS YOU THIS: DO YOU LOVE YOUNG SAT-SAT?

OF COURSE I LOVE MY SON.

AND DO YOU LOVE YOUR FATHER?

AND SO I DO MINE!

YES!

I THOUGHT THOMPSON WAS AT LEAST 40 YEARS OLD. HE COULD EASILY PASS AS MY FATHER.

MY FATHER WAS ON THAT SHIP. PERHAPS IT IS HE WHO HAS SURVIVED!

IF IT IS MY FATHER THAT YOU KILL, THEN...

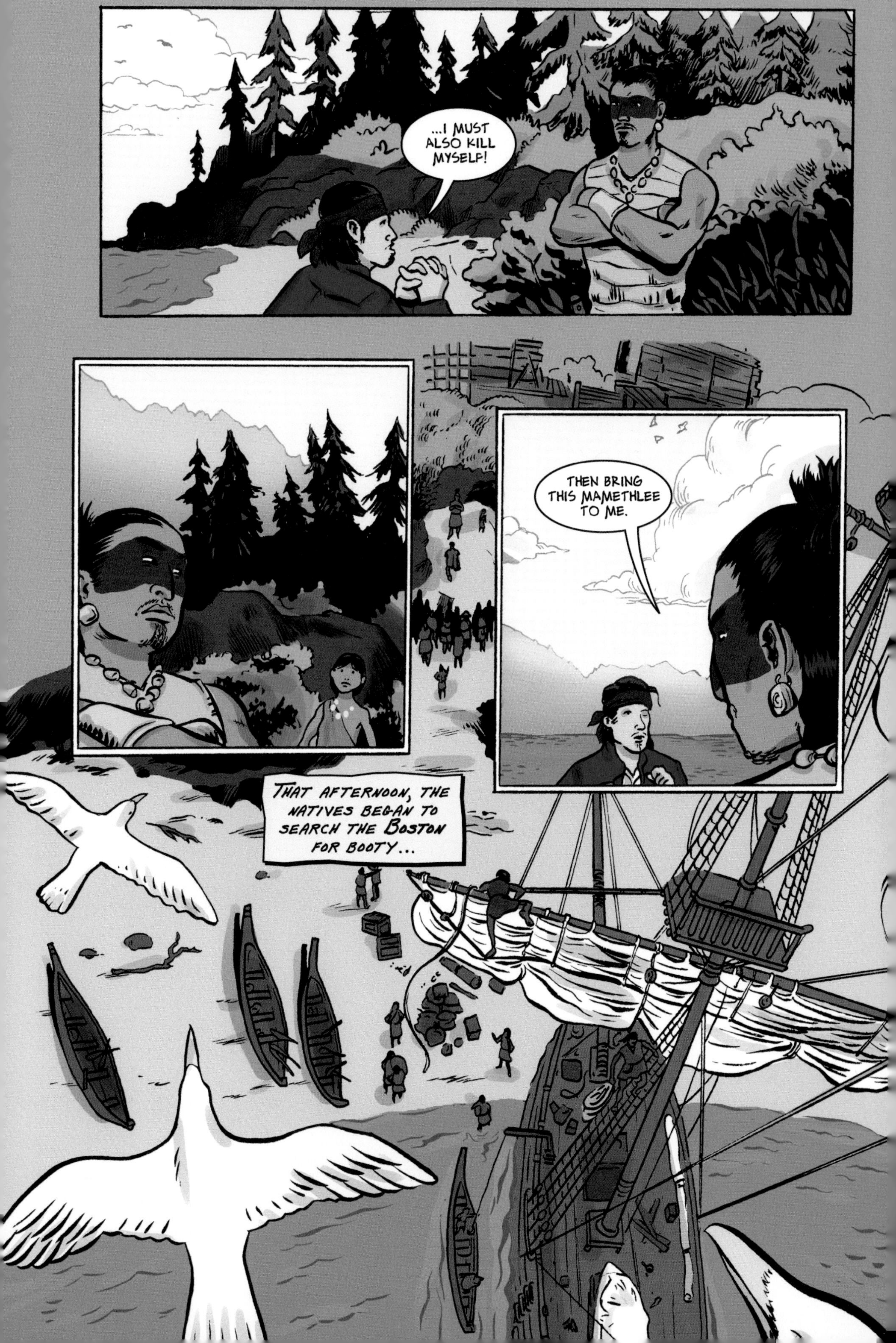
...I MUST ALSO KILL MYSELF!
THEN BRING THIS MAMETHLEE TO ME.
THAT AFTERNOON, THE NATIVES BEGAN TO SEARCH THE BOSTON FOR BOOTY...

...BUT I LOOKED ONLY FOR A MAN...

...A MAN THAT I KNEW.

TO MY UNSPEAKABLE JOY, MY GUESS WAS RIGHT. IT WAS THOMPSON, STILL READY TO FIGHT.

HE HAD HIDDEN IN THE HOLD, HOPING FOR SOME KIND OF ESCAPE.

ALL OUR MEN ARE DEAD.

YOU WILL BE KILLED TOO, UNLESS YOU PRETEND TO BE MY FATHER.

YOU MUST NEVER TELL THE TRUTH!

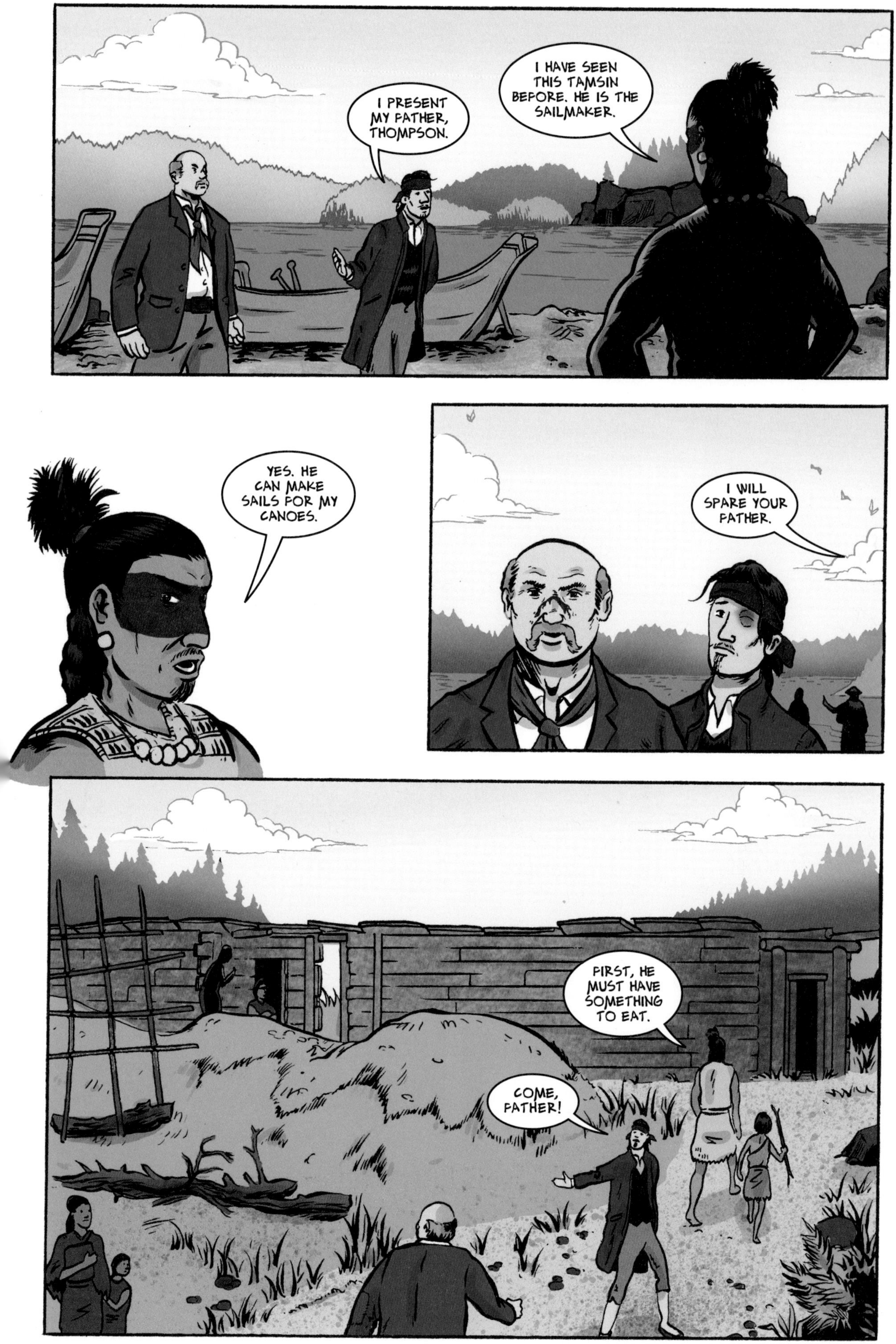
I PRESENT MY FATHER, THOMPSON.
I HAVE SEEN THIS TAMSIN BEFORE. HE IS THE SAILMAKER.
YES. HE CAN MAKE SAILS FOR MY CANOES.
I WILL SPARE YOUR FATHER.
FIRST, HE MUST HAVE SOMETHING TO EAT.
COME, FATHER!

ON MARCH 24, THE NATIVES SEIZED THE WEALTH OF OUR SHIP AND REMOVED IT TO THE CHIEF'S HOUSE. WE WERE FORCED TO HELP THEM.

IT WAS A COMFORT TO BRING FAMILIAR ITEMS ASHORE.

I THOUGHT IT BEST TO SECURE THE SHIP'S ACCOUNTS AND PAPERS, HOPING THAT SOMEDAY I MIGHT RESTORE THEM TO THE PROPER OWNERS.

I HAD THE GOOD FORTUNE TO FIND THE SHIP'S BIBLE AND A BLANK ACCOUNT BOOK.

I THOUGHT I MIGHT BE ABLE TO KEEP A RECORD OF MY CAPTURE...

...DURING A PERIOD THAT I HOPED WOULD BE BRIEF.

The next day, two ships were seen sailing into Friendly Cove.

They were the MARY and JUNO, of Boston.

POOOM!

POK!

POK!

POK!

The natives quickly opened fire.

POK!

POK!

POK!

Both ships were evidently unwilling to approach further.

WE SHOULD HAVE RECEIVED THEM MORE KINDLY...

IF ONLY THEY HAD RECEIVED THEM MORE KINDLY...

...NOW TRADERS WILL NEVER RETURN.

...NOW PERHAPS TRADERS WILL REFUSE TO COME.

WITH GREAT DREAD, I BEGAN TO REALIZE MY CAPTIVITY MIGHT NOT BE BRIEF AFTER ALL.

A FEW DAYS LATER, MAQUINNA WELCOMED A GREAT NUMBER OF CANOES FILLED WITH NATIVES FROM TWENTY TRIBES.

TRIBES FROM THE NORTH...

...AND OTHERS FROM THE SOUTH, WHO WERE BETTER CLAD AND HAD FINER CANOES.

WE HAVE TAKEN THE MAMETHLEE'S SHIP!

BOK! BOK! BOK!

MAQUINNA'S DRUMMING OPENED THE CELEBRATION.

WE HAVE TAKEN THE MAMETHLEE'S GOODS!

I DID NOT KNOW IT THEN, BUT CAPTAIN SALTER'S INSULT WAS SIMPLY THE LAST IN A LONG LINE OF ABUSES THE NOOTKANS HAD SUFFERED FROM WHITE MEN.

WE HAVE EVEN TAKEN THE MAMETHLEE THEMSELVES!

AND WE HAVE AVENGED MANY WRONGS. COME SHARE OUR GREAT VICTORY!

THE PEOPLE FEASTED ON WHALE BLUBBER, SMOKED HERRING SPAWN, AND DRIED FISH MOST PLENTIFULLY.

AND THEN THE ENTERTAINMENT BEGAN.

SAT-SAT-SOK-SIS DANCED...

TOKA, TOKA, TOK, TOKA

AND DANCED...

...AND DANCED.

FOR MORE THAN TWO HOURS HE DANCED, AS THE WOMEN SANG OUT THEIR PRAISE.

IN HIS SON'S HONOR, MAQUINNA BEGAN TO GIVE GIFTS. NO FEWER THAN ONE HUNDRED MUSKETS...

...FOUR HUNDRED YARDS OF CLOTH THEY PRIZED HIGHLY ...THE SAME NUMBER OF LOOKING GLASSES.

AND THUS THE WEALTH OF THE BOSTON WAS DISTRIBUTED.

LATER, THE PEOPLE RETIRED TO THEIR CANOES FOR THE NIGHT.

AND SO IT CONTINUED FOR SEVERAL DAYS.

THEY CALLED THIS GIFT-GIVING CEREMONY A POTLATCH.

IT GREATLY ENHANCED MAQUINNA'S STATUS AMONGST THE TRIBES...

...EVEN AS IT CEMENTED THOMPSON'S AND MINE AS SLAVES. BUT AT LEAST I WAS NO LONGER ALONE IN MY UNHAPPY FATE.

AND VERY SOON, A GREAT INFERNO WOULD SEVER ONCE AND FOR ALL OUR TIES TO THE CIVILIZED WORLD AND OUR LIVES AS FREE MEN.

# CHAPTER 4
## Up in Smoke

MARCH ENDED WITH A DEVASTATING LOSS FOR *THOMPSON* AND ME.

ONE OF THE NATIVES STOLE ONTO THE *BOSTON* IN SEARCH OF PLUNDER.

IT TOOK ONLY A SPARK FROM HIS TORCH...

...TO IGNITE THE COMBUSTIBLES IN THE HOLD.

AND IN MOMENTS OUR SHIP WAS ABLAZE.

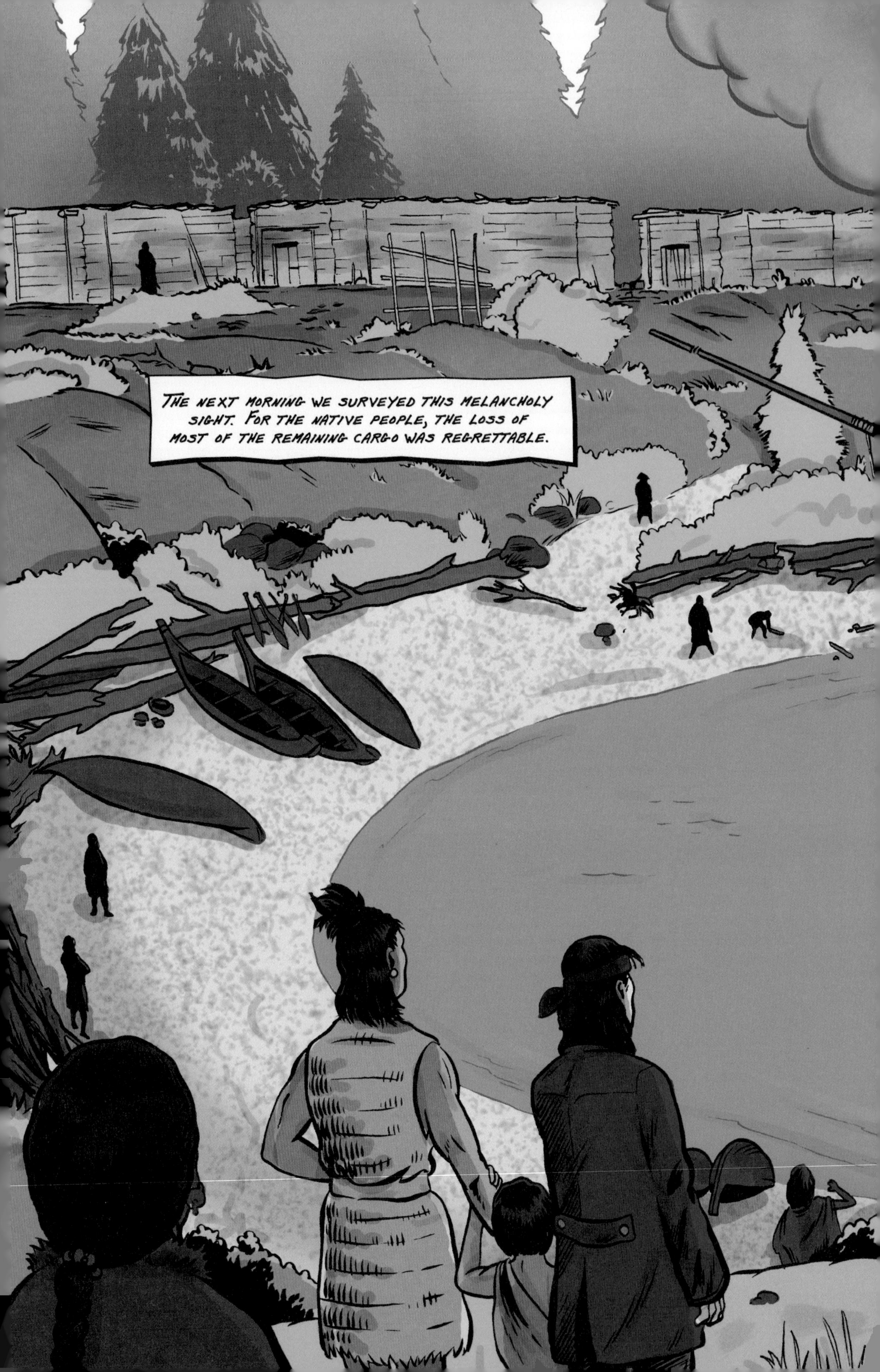
THE NEXT MORNING WE SURVEYED THIS MELANCHOLY SIGHT. FOR THE NATIVE PEOPLE, THE LOSS OF MOST OF THE REMAINING CARGO WAS REGRETTABLE.

FOR THOMPSON AND ME,
IT WAS DISASTROUS.

ALL THE SHIP'S PROVISIONS ARE GONE... AND THE NATIVES WOULD NOT HAVE TOUCHED OUR CURED FOODS—THEY WON'T EAT SALT.

WE COULD HAVE LIVED ON IT FOR YEARS.

BUT HERE IS A BOX OF CHOCOLATE!

AND SOME PORT WINE!

THANKFULLY, I BROUGHT MY TOOLS ASHORE BEFORE THIS TERRIBLE HAPPENING.

ONE MAN CARRIED OFF OUR MURDERED CAPTAIN'S NAUTICAL ALMANAC, BUT HAVING NO USE FOR IT, TRADED IT FOR MY KNIFE.

I HOPED IT WOULD ALLOW ME TO TRACK THE PASSAGE OF TIME, FOR I HAD NO OTHER MEANS AVAILABLE.

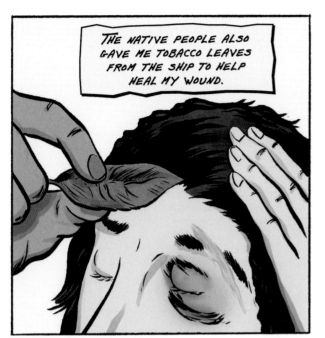

THE NATIVE PEOPLE ALSO GAVE ME TOBACCO LEAVES FROM THE SHIP TO HELP HEAL MY WOUND.

I MUST DO MAQUINNA THE JUSTICE OF SAYING HE ALWAYS TRIED TO SPARE ME ANY LABOR THAT HE BELIEVED MIGHT BE HURTFUL TO ME.

DOES IT STILL PAIN YOU?

AND WHILE I WAS STILL FEEBLE FROM LOSS OF BLOOD, I WAS ABLE TO RESUME SOME WORK AT MY TRADE. I FASHIONED SMALL ORNAMENTS, MANY MADE OF COPPER.

THESE GREATLY PLEASED MAQUINNA AND HIS WOMEN, AND SECURED ME THEIR GOODWILL, WHICH I KNEW MIGHT SOMEDAY SAVE MY LIFE.

47

AND ALL THE WHILE, OTHER TRIBES KEPT FLOCKING TO NOOTKA TO TRADE WHAT WAS LEFT OF THE BOSTON'S PLUNDER.

THEY BROUGHT WITH THEM VAST QUANTITIES OF THEIR OWN SUPPLIES.

AND WITH THEM, CAME AN OPPORTUNITY FOR ME.

MAQUINNA ALLOWED ME TO MAKE COPPER ORNAMENTS, FISHHOOKS, AND DAGGERS FOR THE VISITORS.

Ping!

Ping!

Ping!

Ping!

THEY IN TURN MADE ME GIFTS OF YARDS OF CLOTH, WHICH THOMPSON FASHIONED INTO CLOTHING FOR US.

THEY ALSO SUPPLIED ME WITH AS MUCH SALMON, COD, AND DRIED CLAMS AS I WANTED, AND SOME FOR THOMPSON, AS WELL.

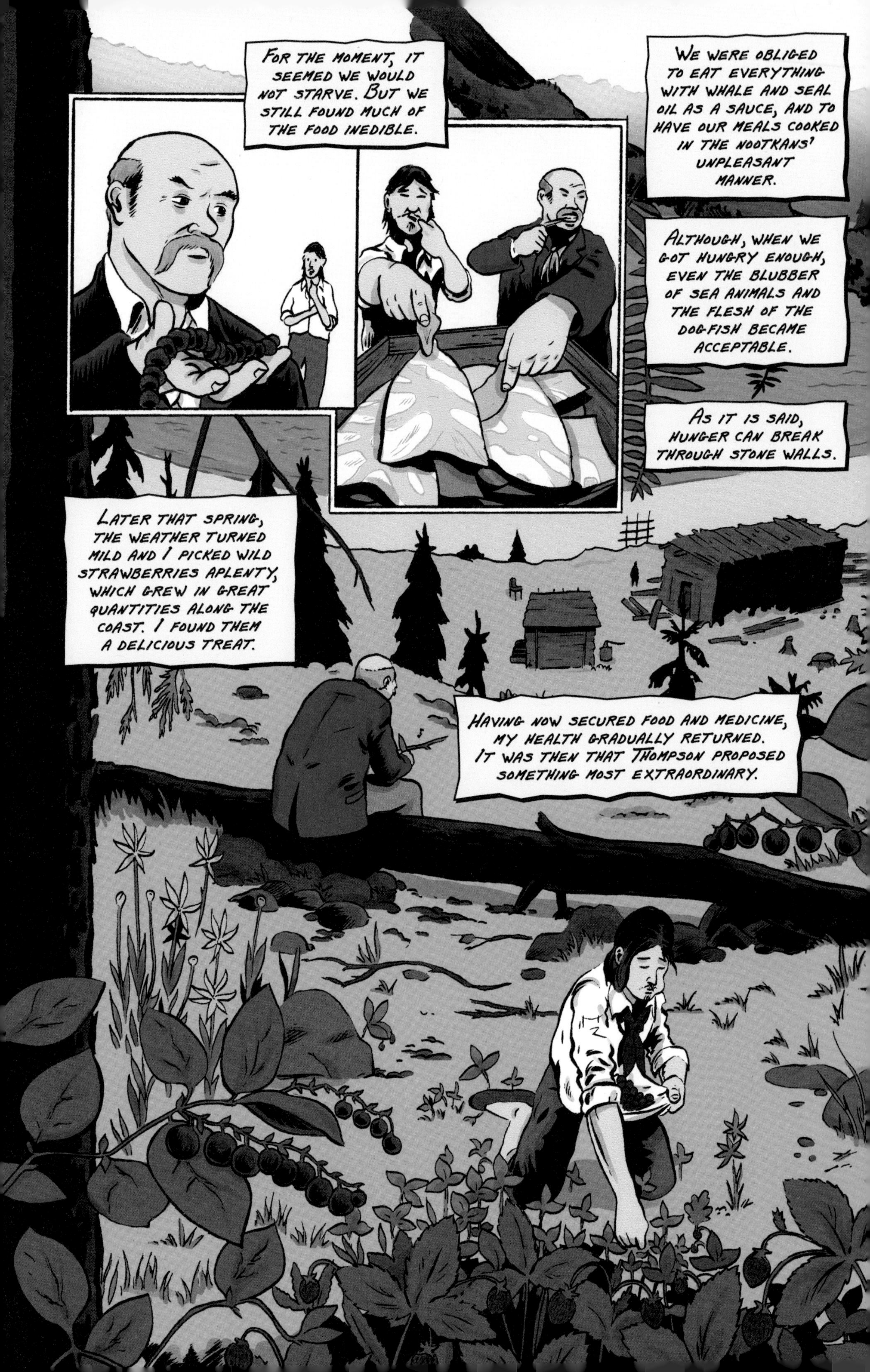
For the moment, it seemed we would not starve. But we still found much of the food inedible.
We were obliged to eat everything with whale and seal oil as a sauce, and to have our meals cooked in the Nootkans' unpleasant manner.
Although, when we got hungry enough, even the blubber of sea animals and the flesh of the dog-fish became acceptable.
As it is said, hunger can break through stone walls.
Later that spring, the weather turned mild and I picked wild strawberries aplenty, which grew in great quantities along the coast. I found them a delicious treat.
Having now secured food and medicine, my health gradually returned. It was then that Thompson proposed something most extraordinary.

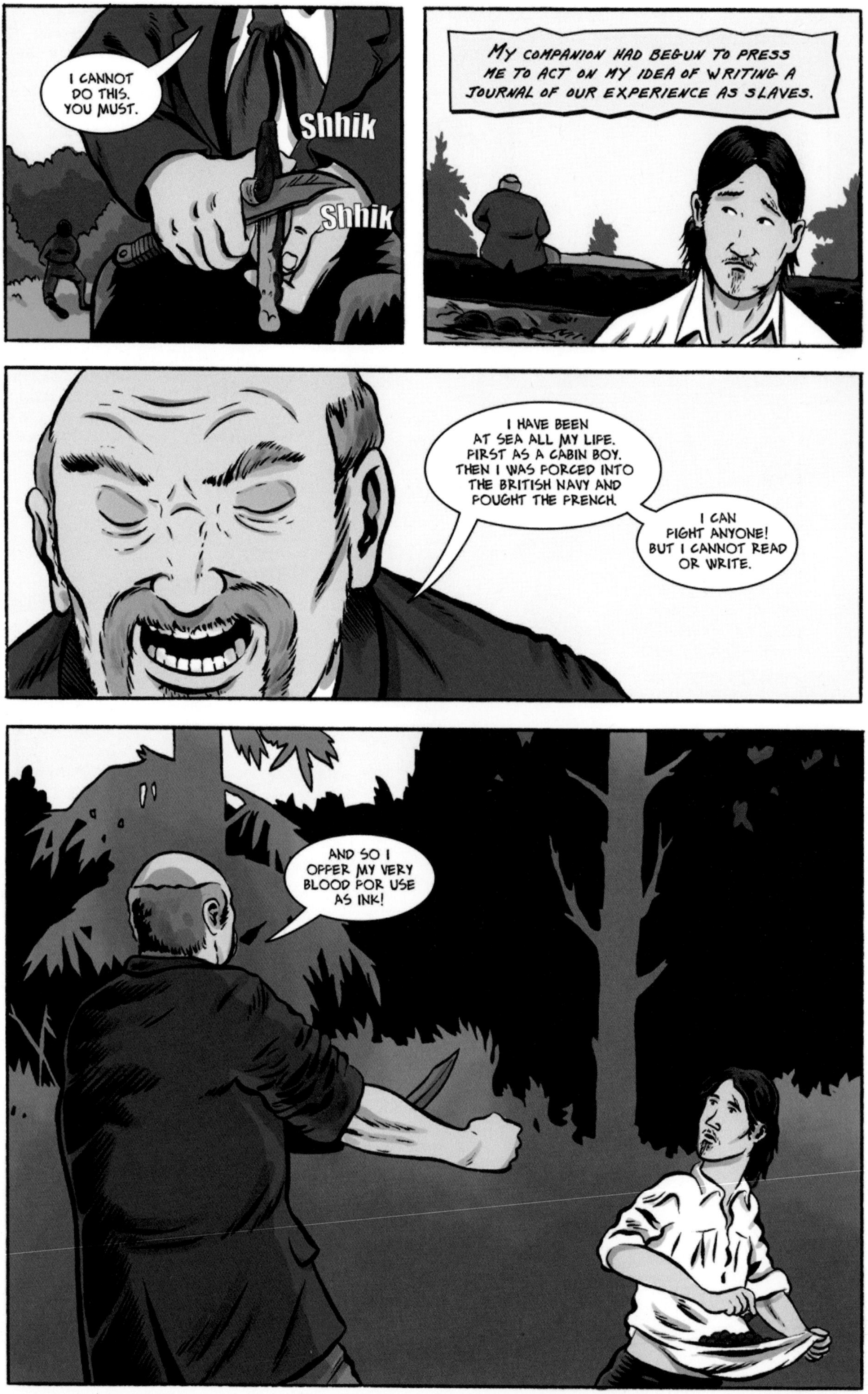
I CANNOT DO THIS. YOU MUST.
Shhik
Shhik
MY COMPANION HAD BEGUN TO PRESS ME TO ACT ON MY IDEA OF WRITING A JOURNAL OF OUR EXPERIENCE AS SLAVES.
I HAVE BEEN AT SEA ALL MY LIFE. FIRST AS A CABIN BOY. THEN I WAS FORCED INTO THE BRITISH NAVY AND FOUGHT THE FRENCH.
I CAN FIGHT ANYONE! BUT I CANNOT READ OR WRITE.
AND SO I OFFER MY VERY BLOOD FOR USE AS INK!

I DID NOT ACCEPT MY COMPANION'S BLOOD OFFERING.

INSTEAD, I LEARNED HOW TO BOIL THE JUICE OF WILD BERRIES AND MIX IT WITH FINELY POWDERED CHARCOAL.

IT WORKED VERY WELL.

AS FOR QUILLS...

...I HAD NO DIFFICULTY PROCURING THEM.

AND SO I BEGAN TO WRITE A REGULAR DIARY — WITH THOMPSON HIMSELF AS ONE OF MY SUBJECTS.

"THOMPSON WAS A VERY STRONG AND POWERFUL MAN, AN EXPERT BOXER."

THOMPSON WAS FEARLESS...

...EVEN RECKLESS.

BIF!

AND HE VERY SOON GAVE ME SOMETHING MOST DREADFUL TO WRITE ABOUT.

IT HAPPENED ONE EVENING, WHEN A YOUNG MAN CAME RUNNING TO ME IN GREAT DISTRESS.

YOU MUST COME! NOW! COME! COME!

THE CHIEF IS ABOUT TO MURDER YOUR FATHER!

!!!

FIRE, I TELL YOU! FIRE!

FIRE!

53

PLEASE, MY CHIEF, DO NOT KILL MY FATHER!

I ADDRESSED HIM IN SOOTHING WORDS.

PLEASE.

I BEG OF YOU, TYEE.

PLEASE.

CAN THIS EVIL-TEMPERED MAN TRULY BE YOUR FATHER?

IF MY FATHER IS KILLED I MUST DO THE SAME TO MYSELF. I HAVE SAID THIS BEFORE.

YOU MUST THEN HAVE RECEIVED YOUR GENTLE NATURE FROM YOUR MOTHER!

AT LENGTH HE ALLOWED ME TO TAKE THE MUSKET FROM HIM AND EXPLAINED THE CAUSE OF HIS FURY.

IT SEEMS THOMPSON HAD BEEN PREPARING THE EVENING LAMPS...

...WHEN SOME OF THE BOYS BEGAN TO TEASE HIM.

FOR THEM IT WAS PLAY.

FOR THOMPSON IT WAS WAR.

YOU LITTLE WRETCHES!

AND SAT-SAT BORE THE BRUNT OF THOMPSON'S RAGE.

BIF!

THE CHIEF WAS IMMEDIATELY INFORMED OF *THOMPSON'S* ASSAULT ON HIS SON.

THIS ACT WAS CONSIDERED TO BE THE HIGHEST INDIGNITY AND A VIOLATION OF A SACRED PERSON.

HAD I ARRIVED A FEW MINUTES LATER, MY COMPANION WOULD HAVE PAID FOR HIS RASH AND VIOLENT CONDUCT WITH HIS LIFE.

AND APPEASING *MAQUINNA* WAS NOT ALL THAT WAS NECESSARY.

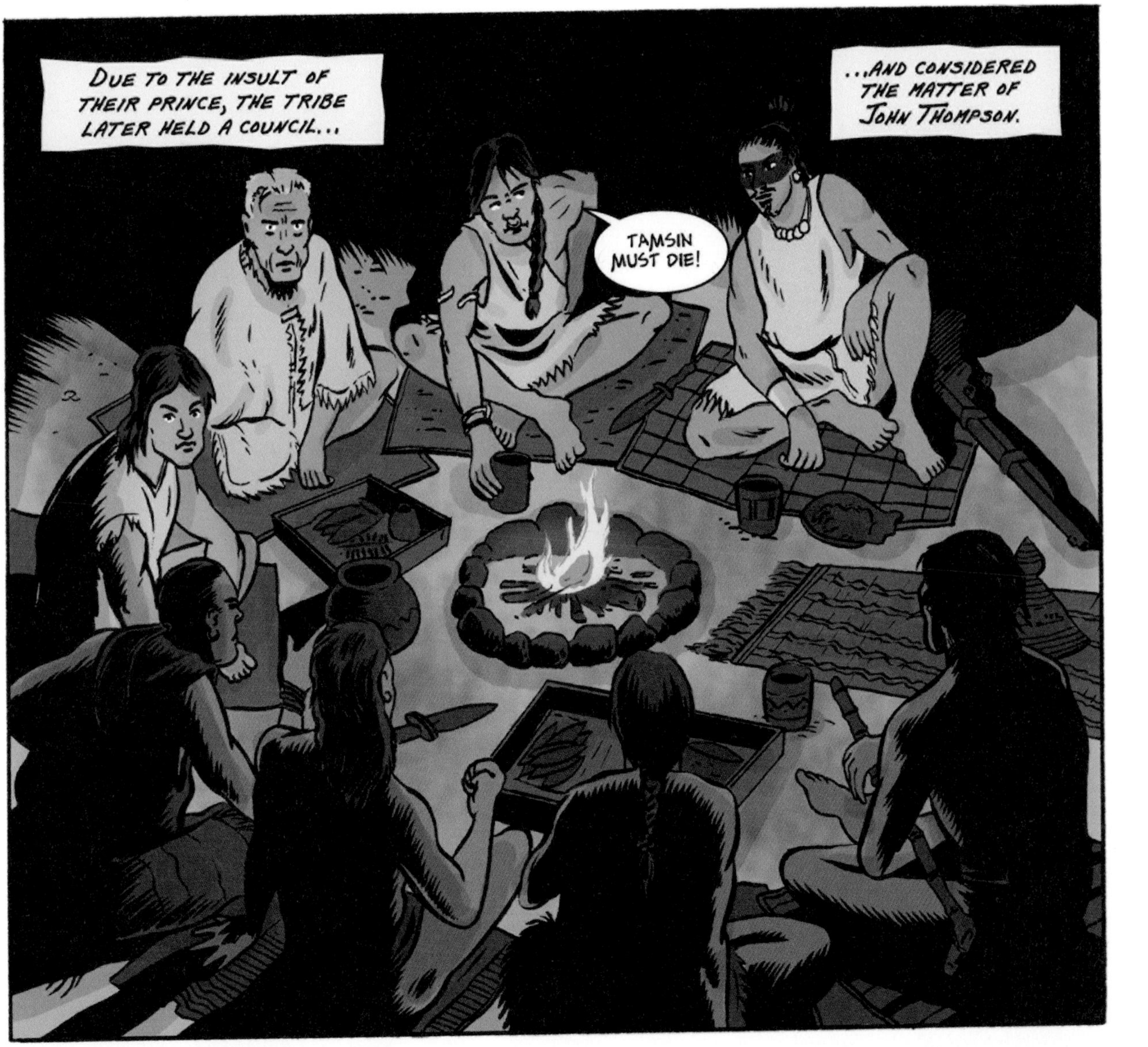
DUE TO THE INSULT OF THEIR PRINCE, THE TRIBE LATER HELD A COUNCIL...
...AND CONSIDERED THE MATTER OF JOHN THOMPSON.
TAMSIN MUST DIE!

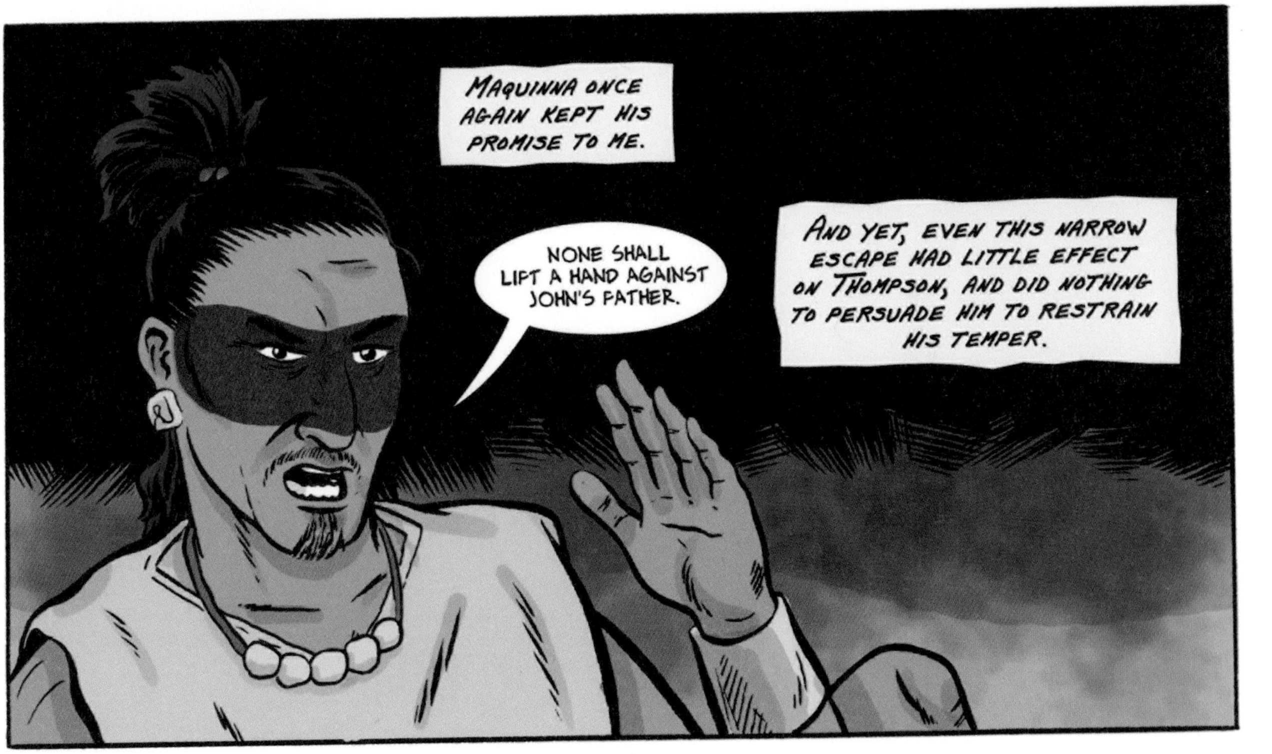
MAQUINNA ONCE AGAIN KEPT HIS PROMISE TO ME.
NONE SHALL LIFT A HAND AGAINST JOHN'S FATHER.
AND YET, EVEN THIS NARROW ESCAPE HAD LITTLE EFFECT ON THOMPSON, AND DID NOTHING TO PERSUADE HIM TO RESTRAIN HIS TEMPER.

A FEW WEEKS LATER, HE LASHED OUT AGAIN, THIS TIME PROVOKED BY THE SON OF ANOTHER CHIEF WHO HAD CALLED HIM A WHITE SLAVE.

WHAM!

IT CAUSED A GREAT COMMOTION IN THE VILLAGE, AND THE TRIBE ONCE AGAIN CLAMORED FOR THOMPSON'S DEATH — AND STILL MAQUINNA WOULD NOT CONSENT TO IT.

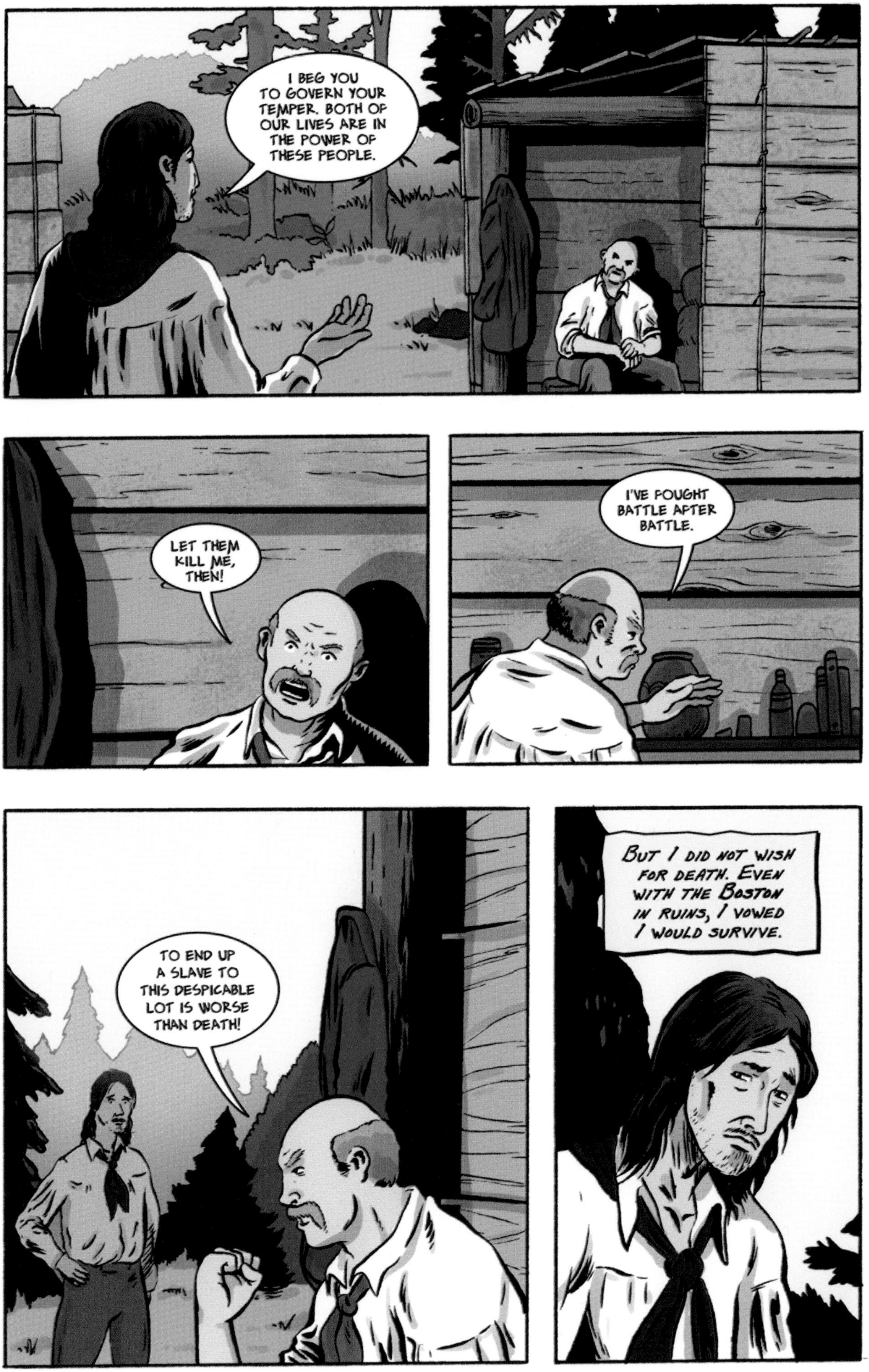
I BEG YOU TO GOVERN YOUR TEMPER. BOTH OF OUR LIVES ARE IN THE POWER OF THESE PEOPLE.
LET THEM KILL ME, THEN!
I'VE FOUGHT BATTLE AFTER BATTLE.
TO END UP A SLAVE TO THIS DESPICABLE LOT IS WORSE THAN DEATH!
BUT I DID NOT WISH FOR DEATH. EVEN WITH THE BOSTON IN RUINS, I VOWED I WOULD SURVIVE.

# CHAPTER 5
## Maquinna's Complaint

I QUICKLY REALIZED THAT TO SURVIVE, I WOULD HAVE TO CONFORM TO THE NOOTKAN PEOPLE'S CUSTOMS AND MODE OF THINKING.

THROUGHOUT THAT SUMMER, I LEARNED MORE OF THE LANGUAGE.

I'M HUNGRY... "HAH-WELKS."

THE PEOPLE CALL THIS PLACE "YUQUOT"...

"YUQUOT."

...WHICH MEANS "WHERE THE WIND BLOWS FROM ALL DIRECTIONS."

I HAD ALWAYS STRUGGLED WITH MY LATIN STUDIES AT HOME, DUE TO A SPEECH IMPEDIMENT.

WE CALL OUR ROBES THE "KUTSAK."

BUT NOW I LEARNED WORDS EVEN MORE FOREIGN TO MY EAR.

"SIE-YAH."

SKY... "SIE-YAH."

THE WORD FOR CLOTH IS "TOOP-HELTH."

?!

I DESPISE THEIR CURSED LINGO. I WANT NOTHING TO DO WITH IT!

I ALSO PAID GREAT ATTENTION TO THEIR MUSIC, WHICH WAS GENERALLY SOFT AND SORROWFUL AND NOT AT ALL DEFICIENT IN HARMONY.

NOW YOU MUST SING ONE OF YOUR SONGS FOR US!

I HAD OFTEN BEEN COMPLIMENTED ON MY OWN SINGING BACK IN ENGLAND.

AHEM.

"WHAT SHALL WE DO WITH A DRUNKEN SAILOR? WHAT SHALL WE DO WITH A DRUNKEN SAILOR?..."

THE NOOTKANS APPEARED PLEASED BY MY VOICE AS WELL.

"...WHAT SHALL WE DO WITH A DRUNKEN SAILOR, EARLY IN THE MORNING!..."

AND IN THIS WAY, I CONTINUED TO GAIN THEIR GOODWILL.

"...HOORAY AND UP SHE RISES, EARLY IN THE MORNING!"

When there was no food at our home, I would often enter others' without ceremony.

In particular, a young chief named Toowinnakinnish was always most kind.

HAH-WELKS. HUNGRY.

COME IN, THEN.

I was never refused.

Few, even amongst nations calling themselves civilized, are as generous as these people, willing as they are to deprive themselves of food for a stranger.

THEIR FOOD CONSISTS ALMOST WHOLLY OF FISH, FISH SPAWN, WHALE AND SEAL BLUBBER, MUSSELS, CLAMS, AND BERRIES...

...ALL DOUSED IN WHALE OIL, WHICH THEY RENDER FROM THE BLUBBER.

THIS NOURISHMENT KEEPS THEM STRONG AND I HAVE NOTICED VERY LITTLE ILLNESS EXCEPT FOR COLIC AND RHEUMATISM.

THE MEN ARE ABOUT FIVE FEET SIX TO FIVE FEET EIGHT...

...REMARKABLY STRAIGHT, OF GOOD FORM...

...ROBUST AND POWERFUL.

AS FOR THE WOMEN, THEY ARE IN GENERAL WELL LOOKING — AND SOME QUITE HANDSOME.

THEY ARE EXTREMELY MODEST IN THEIR APPEARANCE.

THOUGH THE WOMEN ARE FOND OF ORNAMENTING THEMSELVES...

...HERE, IT IS THE MEN WHO ARE MOST PARTIAL TO FACE PAINT.

SOMETIMES THE MEN LAID ON THEIR FACE A THICK LAYER OF BEAR GREASE, WHICH THEY RAISED INTO RIDGES AND PAINTED RED, GIVING A VERY SINGULAR APPEARANCE.

I HAVE KNOWN MAQUINNA TO PASS MORE THAN AN HOUR PAINTING HIS FACE, ONLY TO RUB THE WHOLE OF IT OFF AND START ANEW IF IT DID NOT ENTIRELY PLEASE HIM.

THE ORNAMENT THE MEN VALUE MOST IS THE NOSE-JEWEL...

...IF SUCH A NAME MAY BE GIVEN TO A BIT OF COPPER OR A WOODEN STICK!

I HAVE SEEN THESE ORNAMENTS PROJECTING EIGHT OR NINE INCHES ON EITHER SIDE OF THE FACE...

...SECURED BY A SMALL WEDGE ON EACH SIDE.

HAH!

THOMPSON, AS USUAL, MADE THE PEOPLE VERY ANGRY.

HA, HA!

OF COURSE, THOMPSON HAD NO INTEREST IN CULTIVATING THEIR FAVOR.

BUT THOMPSON'S INSULTS, I LEARNED, WERE NOTHING COMPARED TO THE ABUSES OF EARLIER WHITE VISITORS...

...SUCH AS THE INFAMOUS CAPTAIN TAWNINGTON.

TAWNINGTON STAYED HERE ONE WINTER AND WAS TREATED WITH GREAT KINDNESS.

"ONE DAY, I WENT AWAY TO SEEK A WIFE AND LEFT THE WOMEN ALONE."

"THE CAPTAIN AND HIS MEN WASTED NO TIME RANSACKING MY HOME."

"THEY STOLE ALL THE SKINS THERE— FORTY OF MY BEST."

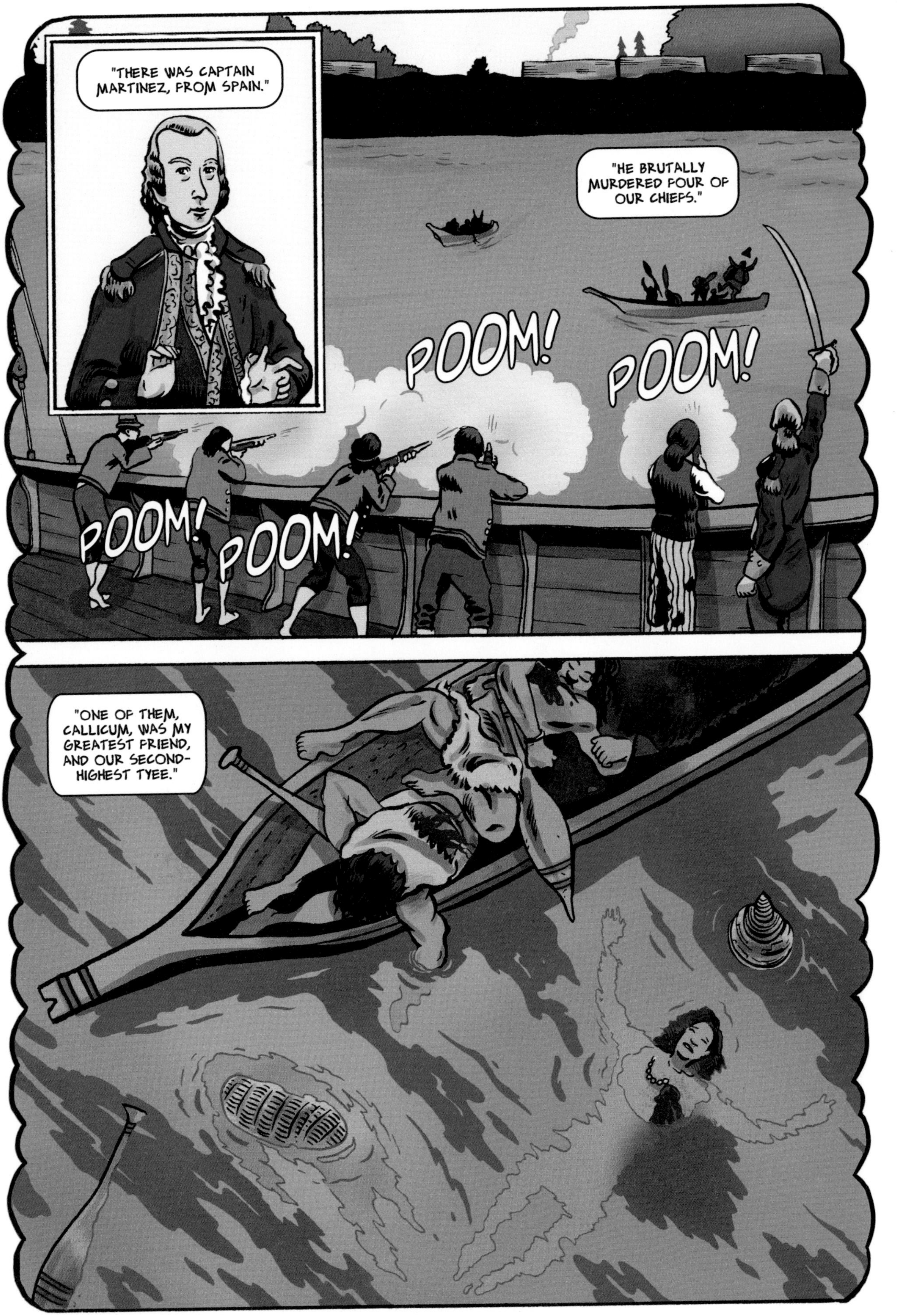
"THERE WAS CAPTAIN MARTINEZ, FROM SPAIN."
"HE BRUTALLY MURDERED FOUR OF OUR CHIEFS."
POOM!
POOM!
POOM!
POOM!
"ONE OF THEM, CALLICUM, WAS MY GREATEST FRIEND, AND OUR SECOND-HIGHEST TYEE."

AND ONE WAS MORE TERRIBLE YET...

"JAMES HANNA, CAPTAIN OF THE SEA-OTTER. ONE DAY HE DISCOVERED A NATIVE HAD STOLEN A CARPENTER'S CHISEL..."

"...AND SO HE TOOK HIS REVENGE."

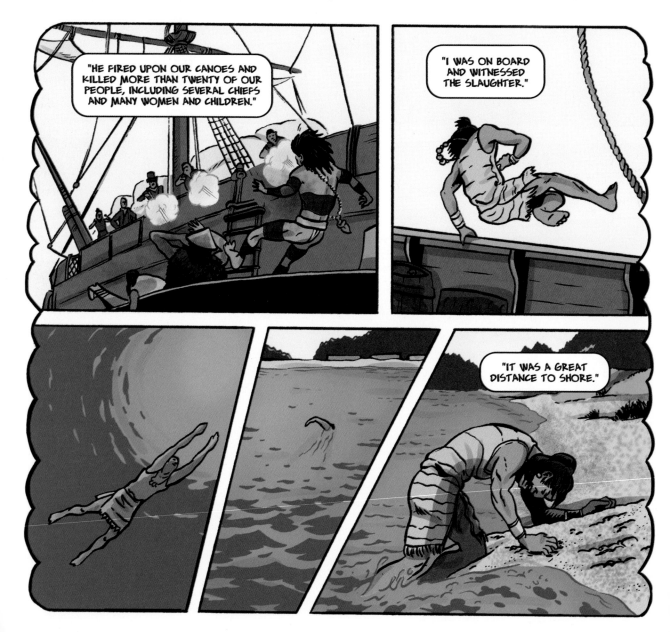

"HE FIRED UPON OUR CANOES AND KILLED MORE THAN TWENTY OF OUR PEOPLE, INCLUDING SEVERAL CHIEFS AND MANY WOMEN AND CHILDREN."

"I WAS ON BOARD AND WITNESSED THE SLAUGHTER."

"IT WAS A GREAT DISTANCE TO SHORE."

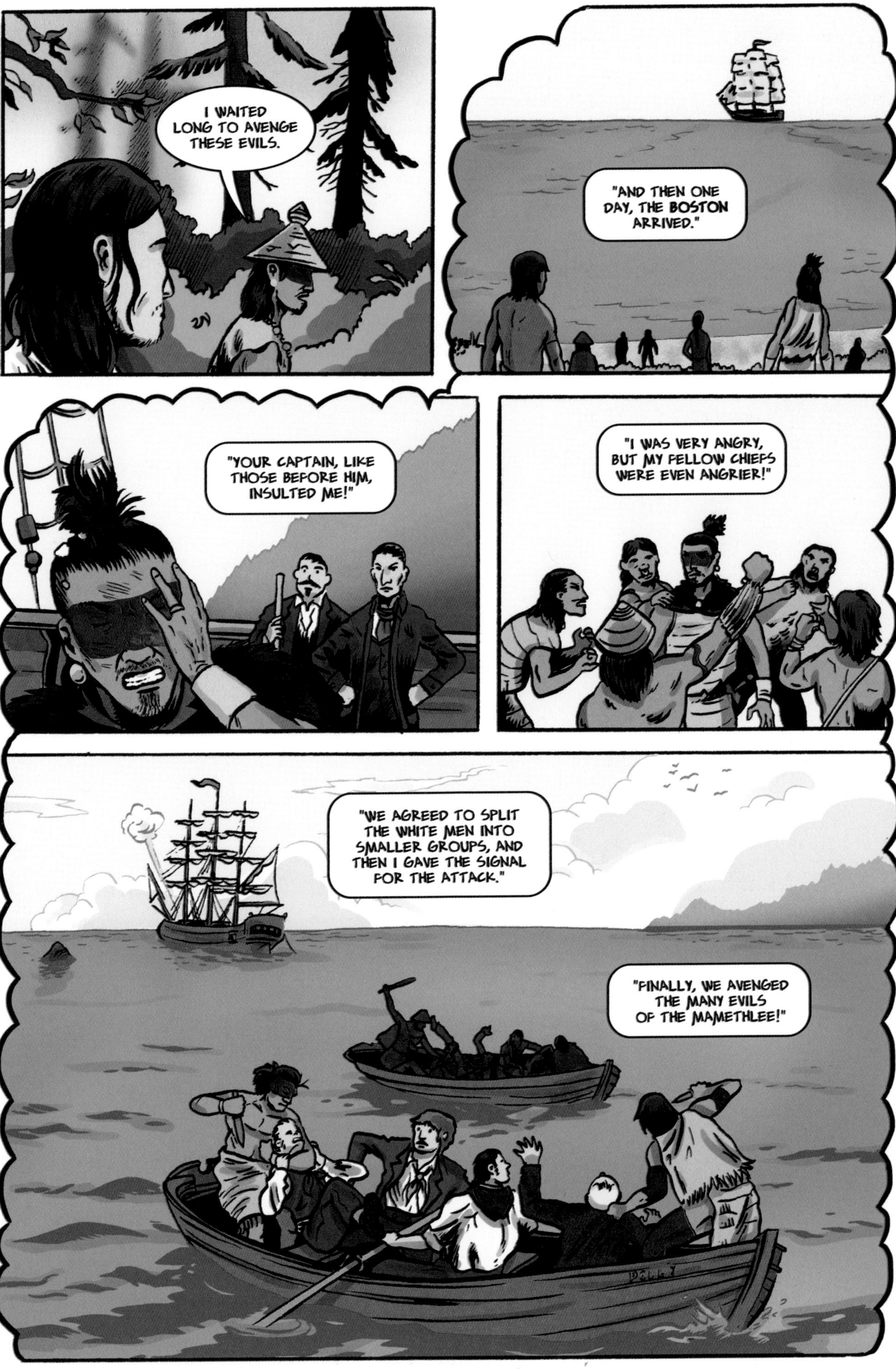

I WAITED LONG TO AVENGE THESE EVILS.
"AND THEN ONE DAY, THE BOSTON ARRIVED."
"YOUR CAPTAIN, LIKE THOSE BEFORE HIM, INSULTED ME!"
"I WAS VERY ANGRY, BUT MY FELLOW CHIEFS WERE EVEN ANGRIER!"
"WE AGREED TO SPLIT THE WHITE MEN INTO SMALLER GROUPS, AND THEN I GAVE THE SIGNAL FOR THE ATTACK."
"FINALLY, WE AVENGED THE MANY EVILS OF THE MAMETHLEE!"

I BECAME CONVINCED THAT IF THOSE EARLIER CAPTAINS AND CREWS HAD BEHAVED BETTER, I'D HAVE BEEN SPARED MY FATE AS A CAPTIVE ON THIS REMOTE ISLAND.

LATE THAT SUMMER, THOUGH...

...AT LAST!

A SHIP APPEARED ON THE HORIZON!

THEIR CRUELTY HAD ONLY EXCITED A DESIRE FOR REVENGE, WHICH IS A POWERFUL PASSION IN THESE PEOPLE'S HEARTS.

AND NOW I WAS FORCED TO SUFFER FOR THE WRONGS OF THE GUILTY ONES...

...FOR THOUGH WE SEARCHED MOST FERVENTLY, THE ATTACK ON THE BOSTON APPEARED TO HAVE DRIVEN OTHER TRADERS AWAY.

BUT OUR FOND HOPES OF RESCUE VANISHED.

INSTEAD OF STANDING IN FOR SHORE, SHE PASSED TO THE NORTH AND SOON DISAPPEARED FROM OUR SIGHT.

SHORTLY AFTER WE SAW THE SHIP PASS, MY LIFE AS A CAPTIVE GREW EVEN WORSE. A TIME OF HUNGER SOON SET IN FOR ALL. THIS TIME, I COULD NOT TURN TO ANOTHER HOUSE FOR HELP.

HUNGRY AS WE WERE, FOOD THAT ONCE DISGUSTED US NOW SEEMED DELICIOUS.

ONE OF THE MEN TOOK US TO A GARDEN THE SPANISH HAD PLANTED DURING THE DAYS THEY HAD CLAIMED FRIENDLY COVE FOR THEMSELVES.

THEY HAD QUIT THEIR CLAIM TO THE LAND AND LEFT EIGHT YEARS EARLIER.

BUT THEIR TURNIPS AND ONIONS STILL GREW WILD.

THESE WERE OUR VERY LAST SMALL TASTES OF CIVILIZATION.

BUT SOON EVEN THIS WOULD BE DENIED US.

WE WERE INFORMED THAT THE WHOLE TRIBE WOULD SHORTLY MOVE TO ITS AUTUMN VILLAGE AT THE HEAD OF AN INLET, THIRTY MILES DEEPER INTO THE WILDERNESS...

...WHERE NEITHER SPANISH GARDENS NOR RESCUE WOULD BE FOUND.

# CHAPTER 6
## The Kidnapping

TODAY THE AIR RESOUNDED WITH THE PEOPLE'S SONGS AS THEY DISMANTLED AND PACKED THEIR ENTIRE VILLAGE.

WE DEPARTED FRIENDLY COVE FOR A PLACE THEY CALL TASHEES, WHERE THEY PASS THE AUTUMN SEASON.

BOSTON

THOMPSON HAD REPAIRED AND FURNISHED OUR LONG-BOAT WITH SAILS. WE NOW WERE COMMANDED TO SAIL NORTH.

THOMPSON AND I QUIT NOOTKA WITH HEAVY HEARTS...

WE SAILED MANY HOURS ALONG AN INLET, KNOWING WELL THAT NO RESCUE SHIP WOULD COME HERE.

YET WHEN WE ARRIVED, I COULD NOT DENY THE BEAUTY OF THE PLACE.

THE VILLAGE WAS LOCATED IN AN AREA SECURE FROM WINTER STORMS.

WE ALL IMMEDIATELY WENT TO WORK COVERING LAST YEAR'S HOUSE FRAMES WITH PLANKS WE HAD BROUGHT.

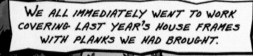

BUT THE SITUATION HERE WAS MORE CONFINED AND WE SORELY FELT THE LACK OF ROOM.

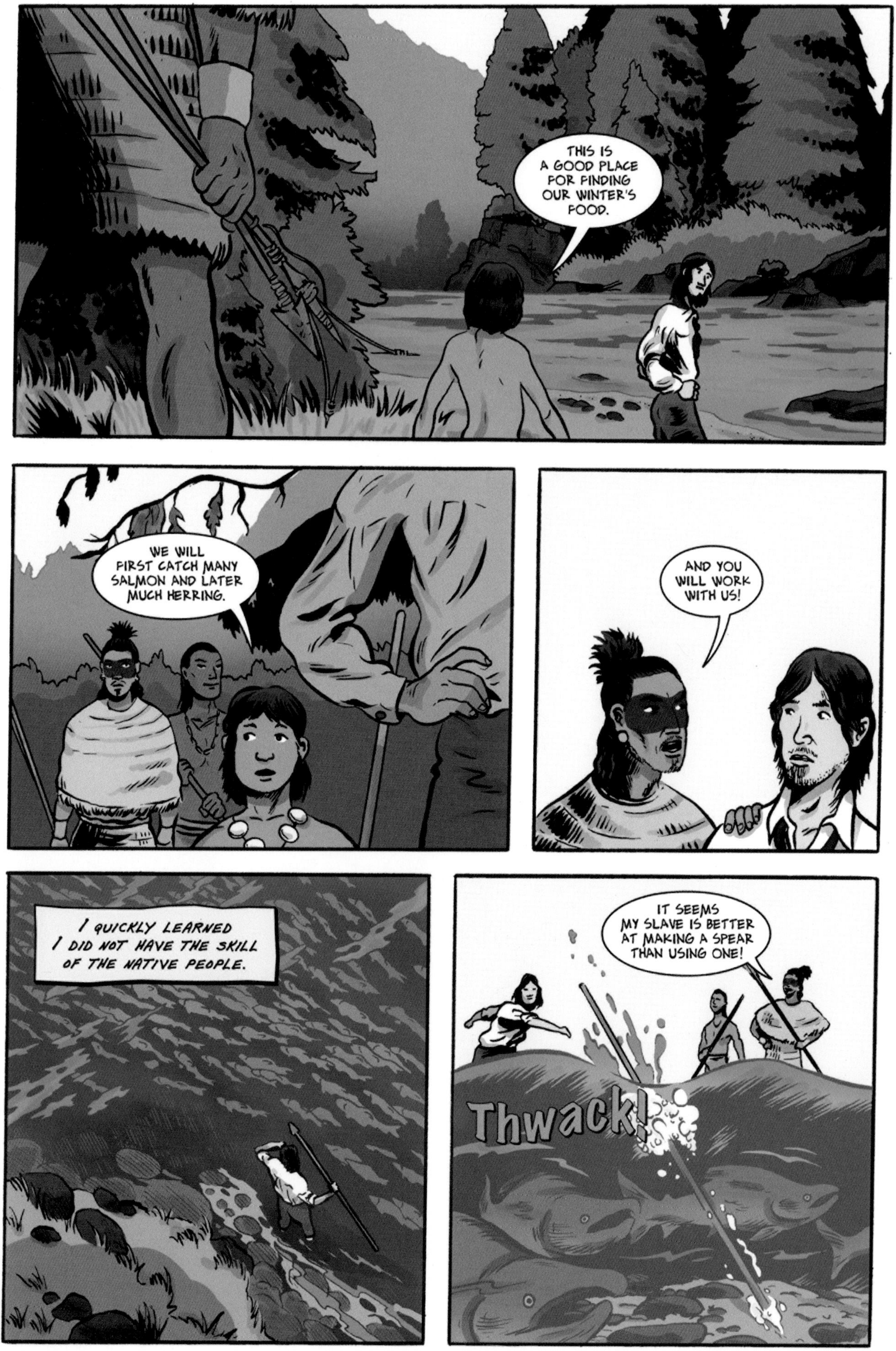
THIS IS A GOOD PLACE FOR FINDING OUR WINTER'S FOOD.
WE WILL FIRST CATCH MANY SALMON AND LATER MUCH HERRING.
AND YOU WILL WORK WITH US!
I QUICKLY LEARNED I DID NOT HAVE THE SKILL OF THE NATIVE PEOPLE.
IT SEEMS MY SLAVE IS BETTER AT MAKING A SPEAR THAN USING ONE!
Thwack!

IT WAS HERE IN TASHEES THAT MAQUINNA DISCOVERED MY JOURNAL.

WHAT DO YOU WRITE, JOHN?

I WAS WRITING ABOUT THE... THE... WEATHER.

MAYBE YOU WRITE BAD THINGS.

YES, BAD THINGS ABOUT ME. ABOUT THE FATE OF YOUR SHIP AND THE CREW. TO TELL YOUR PEOPLE.

IF I SEE YOU WRITING AGAIN, I WILL THROW YOUR PAPERS INTO THE FIRE!

I WAS GRATEFUL THAT MAQUINNA DID NO MORE THAN THREATEN. BUT I BECAME VERY CAUTIOUS AFTERWARD THAT HE NOT OBSERVE MY WRITING AGAIN.

I shall continue to avail myself of every opportunity to write while he is fishing.

LATER, I FINISHED SOME DAGGERS FOR HIM, WHICH I POLISHED HIGHLY. THESE PLEASED HIM MUCH.

MAQUINNA WAS A MAN OF MANY MOODS. SOON HIS ANGER PASSED.

HE, IN FACT, REWARDED MY WORK GENEROUSLY.

AS FOR THOMPSON...

DUE TO HIS SKILL IN MAKING CLOTH SAILS AND GARMENTS, HE BECAME MORE OF A FAVORITE THAN HE FORMERLY HAD BEEN.

VERY FINE, TAMSIN!

Throughout that fall, the people had great success fishing; I have seen more than 700 salmon caught in the space of fifteen minutes. I could eat my fill once again.

And then in early December, the men trapped a truly fearsome beast.

The slain black bear was taken inside, seated opposite Maquinna, crowned with a chief's bonnet, and with great respect, invited to eat.

The people call this "Dressing the Bear" and it is the cause of a great feast and rejoicing.

As usual, Sat-Sat closed the celebration with a dance, though on this occasion he repeatedly shifted his mask from one form into another.

BOOM!

THERE OCCURRED SOON AFTER THIS AN EVEN MORE EXTRAORDINARY DRAMA.

IT SEEMED SAT-SAT HAD BEEN MORTALLY WOUNDED... BY HIS OWN FATHER!

WHAT HAS HAPPENED?

AIYEE!

IT IS THE PRINCE!

AND THEN, WITH THE ARRIVAL OF TWO MEN ON HANDS AND FEET IN THE MANNER OF A BEAST...

...KIDNAPPED!

TAKE THESE PROVISIONS AND LEAVE. GO!

WE WERE BARRED FROM THE EVENTS THAT FOLLOWED SAT-SAT'S SHOCKING ABDUCTION, BUT WERE LEFT FREE TO EXPLORE THE COUNTRYSIDE, WHICH WE FOUND TO BE FILLED WITH BEAUTIFUL HILLS, VALLEYS, AND THE FINEST OF STREAMS.

I CAN MAKE NO SENSE OF WHAT HAS JUST HAPPENED...

WHEN WE WERE FINALLY ALLOWED TO RETURN, THIS MYSTERIOUS EVENT WAS ALL BUT OVER.

SAT-SAT APPEARED TO BE QUITE SAFE. HE HAD SOMEHOW BEEN RESCUED FROM THE SUPERNATURAL WOLF-SPIRIT AND THEN CEREMONIALLY PURIFIED. THEY CALLED THIS THE "WOLF DANCE."

IT WAS PART OF THE NOOTKAN WINTER CEREMONIALS, WHICH ENDED WITH A MOST REMARKABLE DISPLAY OF ENDURANCE.

DESPITE THE AGONY OF SELF-INFLICTED WOUNDS, THE MEN REJOICED IN THEIR SHOW OF COURAGE, PERFORMED IN HONOR OF THEIR GOD, WHOM THEY CALL QUAHOOTZE.

BUT MY THOUGHTS TURNED TO MY OWN GOD WHEN CHRISTMAS ARRIVED.

I COULD ONLY THINK OF MY OWN PEOPLE, NOW ASSEMBLED AND PRAISING OUR SAVIOR.

WITH THE CHIEF'S PERMISSION, WE TWO HELD OUR OWN CEREMONY AND FERVENTLY PRAYED WE WOULD SOMEDAY CELEBRATE CHRISTMAS AT HOME.

"HARK THE HERALD ANGELS SING..."

WE DID WHAT WE COULD TO SHARE A CHRISTMAS DINNER OF SOME DRIED CLAMS, ALONG WITH AN AGREEABLE ROOT CALLED "KLETSUP."

BUT IT WAS NOTHING AT ALL LIKE BEING HOME.

NOTHING.

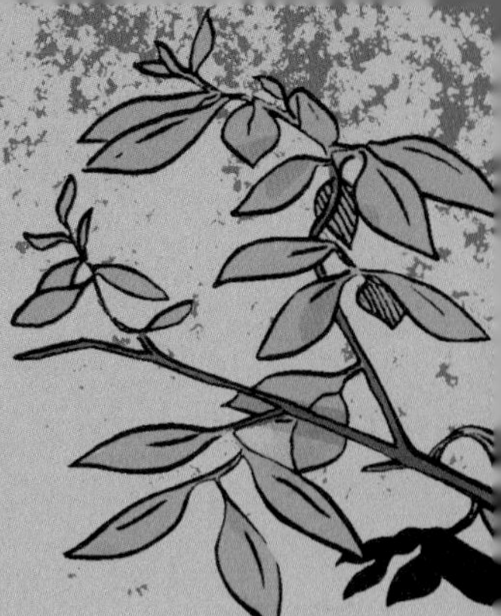

# CHAPTER 7
## The Haunting

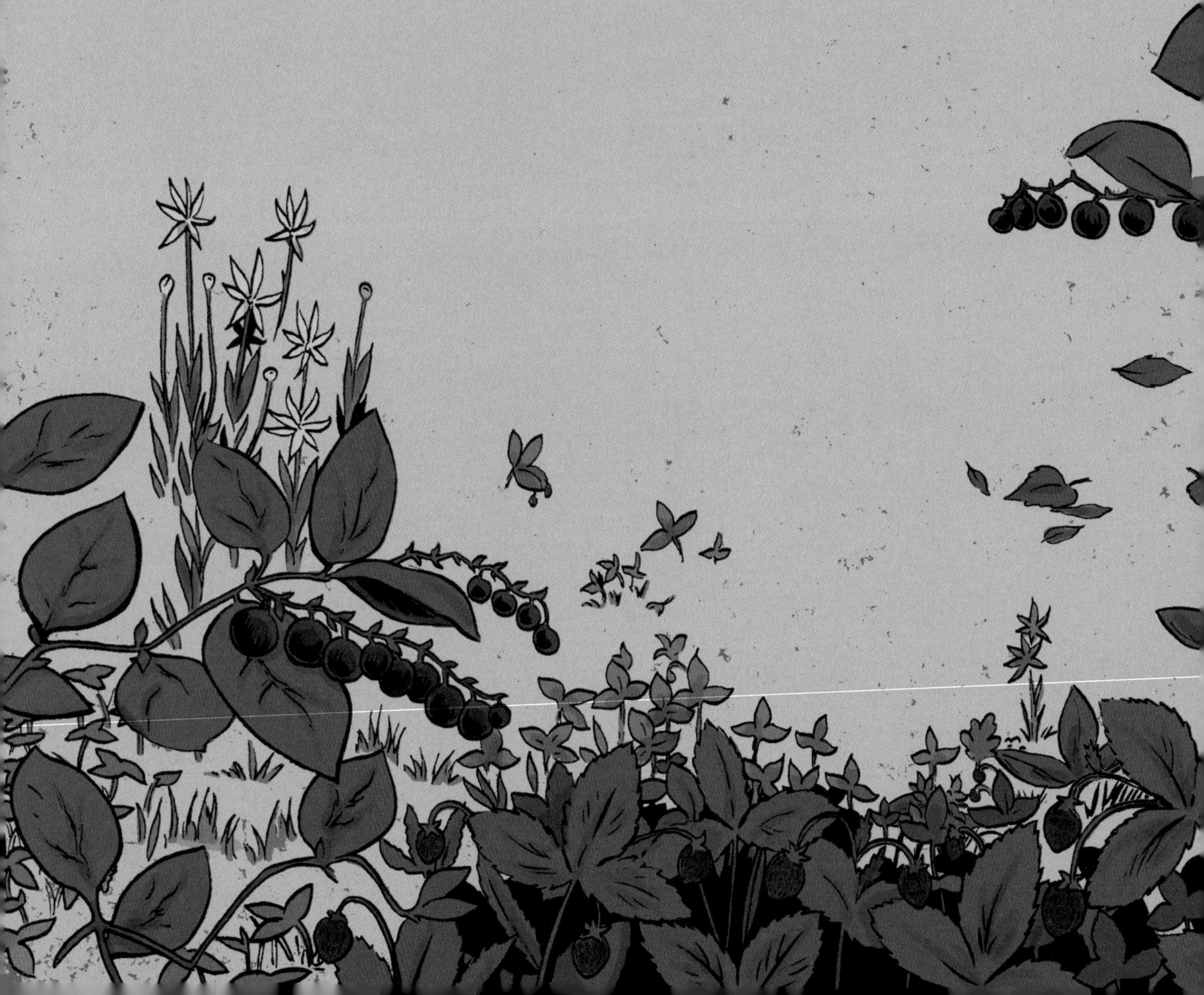

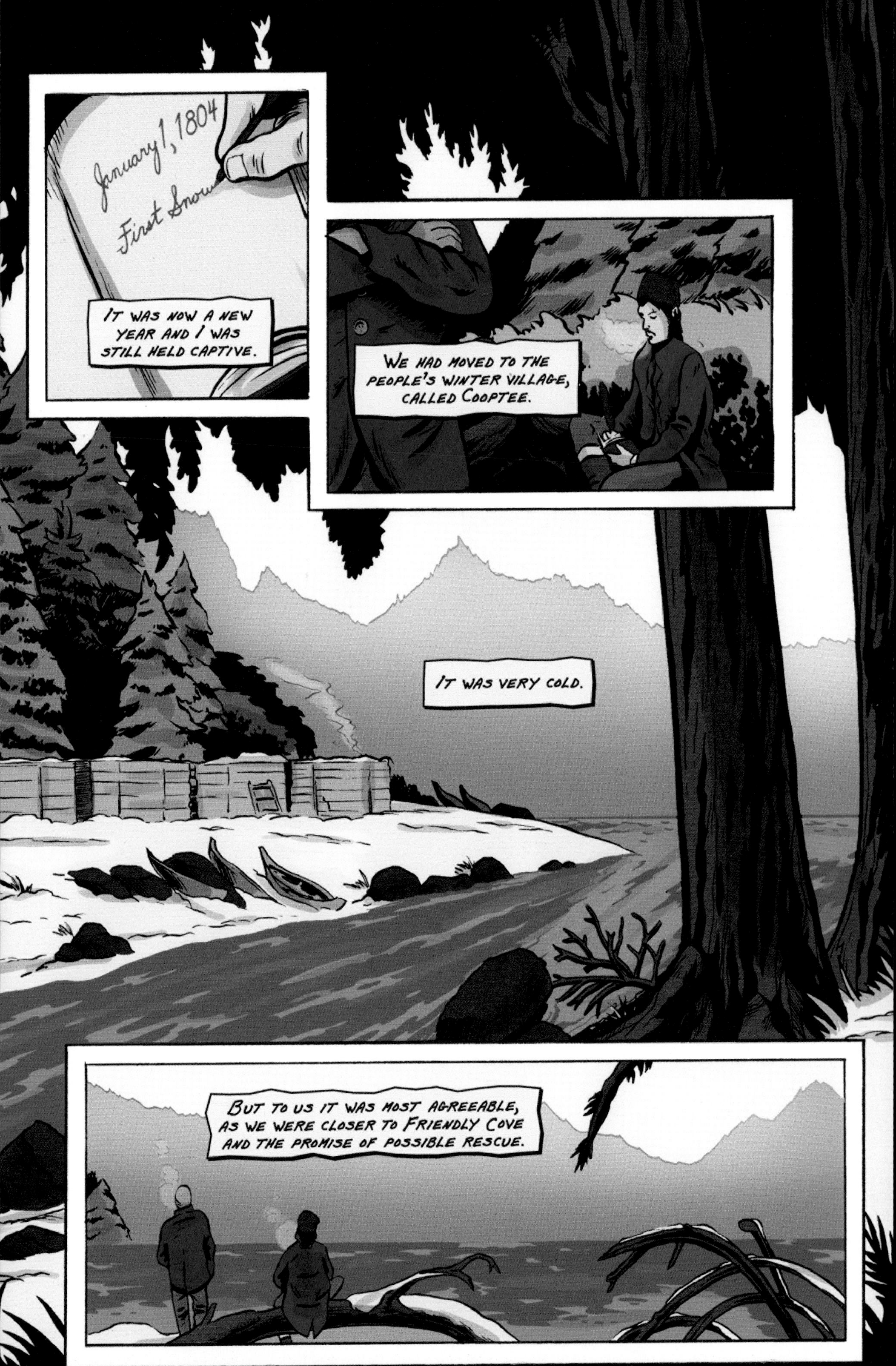
January 1, 1804
First Snow
It was now a new year and I was still held captive.
We had moved to the people's winter village, called Cooptee.
It was very cold.
But to us it was most agreeable, as we were closer to Friendly Cove and the promise of possible rescue.

WOCASH.

WOCASH.

WOCASH.

ONLY A WEEK AFTER OUR MOVE, MAQUINNA TOOK ME FAR UP THE SOUND TO VISIT UPQUESTA, CHIEF OF THE AI-TIZ-ZARTS, WHO WELCOMED US WARMLY.

THE PEOPLE FOUND ME TO BE AN OBJECT OF CURIOSITY. MANY OF THEM HAD NEVER SEEN A WHITE MAN BEFORE.

THEY PEERED INTO MY MOUTH TO SEE IF I HAD A TONGUE...

...AS MAQUINNA HAD FORBIDDEN ME TO SPEAK YET.

AND THEY DISLIKED MY CLOTHING, WHICH, BEING BLUE, MADE ME LOOK SEAL-LIKE TO THEM.

I REMAINED SILENT AS I HAD BEEN ORDERED.

AND THEN, WHEN MAQUINNA GAVE ME A SIGNAL TO SPEAK, I INTRODUCED MYSELF.

OOK-KLA-SISH JOHN JEWITT.*

*MY NAME IS JOHN JEWITT.

THIS SLAVE CAME FROM OUR VICTORY OVER THE BOSTON, WHEN WE AVENGED MANY INSULTS.

THOUGH HE IS WHITE AND RESEMBLES A SEAL IT SEEMS HE IS A MAN AFTER ALL.

(AND A MAN NEEDS A WOMAN.)

AFTER WE HAD BEEN WELL-FED AND ENTERTAINED FOR SOME DAYS, WE DEPARTED FOR HOME ONCE AGAIN. I COULD ONLY WONDER WHY MAQUINNA HAD TAKEN ME ON THIS VOYAGE.

I FOUND THEM TO BE AMONG THE MOST HANDSOME PEOPLE ON THE COAST, AND THE MOST HOSPITABLE AS WELL.

SOON ENOUGH, THOUGH, I WOULD DISCOVER HIS INTENTIONS — AND I WOULD BE GREATLY UNSETTLED BY WHAT I LEARNED.

89

AFTER OUR RETURN TO COOPTEE, MAQUINNA'S PEOPLE BEGAN TO GATHER FOOD FOR A DISPLAY OF HIS OWN HOSPITALITY.

THEY TOOK HERRING AND SPRAT IN GREAT QUANTITIES...

...AS MANY AS TEN TO TWELVE FISH AT A SINGLE STROKE.

WHEN ALL HAD BEEN READIED, MAQUINNA HELD HIS GREAT ANNUAL ENTERTAINMENT, WELCOMING HIS OWN PEOPLE, 100 AI-TIZ-ZARTS, AND MANY OTHERS FROM WICKINNINISH. THERE WERE COMPETITIONS...

...AND AN ASTONISHING QUANTITY OF FOOD. ON THIS OCCASION I SAW UPWARD OF 100 SALMON COOKED IN ONE TUB ALONE.

THEY ATE ALL THEY HAD AND SEEMED TO HAVE LITTLE WORRY ABOUT LEAN TIMES THAT MIGHT LIE AHEAD. FOR THEM, WINTER WAS A TIME OF COMMUNITY AND CELEBRATION.

IN LATE FEBRUARY, AS THE SEASON OF GREAT FEASTING DREW TO A CLOSE, WE QUITTED COOPTEE AND RETURNED TO FRIENDLY COVE.

WITH MUCH JOY, THOMPSON AND I FOUND OURSELVES BACK IN A PLACE WHERE THERE MIGHT ARRIVE A VESSEL TO OUR RESCUE.

BUT THERE WAS ONE MAN WHO WOULD FIND ONLY GRIEF WAITING FOR HIM IN FRIENDLY COVE.

HE WAS NAMED TATOOSCH, AND WAS BROTHER-IN-LAW TO MAQUINNA. TATOOSCH HAD A MUCH-BELOVED SON WHO HAD FALLEN ILL.

TATOOSCH WAS ESTEEMED AS THE FIRST WARRIOR OF THE TRIBE. INDEED, HE HAD BEEN PARTICULARLY ACTIVE IN THE DESTRUCTION OF OUR SHIP.

HE'D KILLED MY COMRADE, JOHN HALL.

AND HE'D KILLED ANOTHER, SAMUEL WOOD. BOTH MEN HAD BEEN ASHORE AT THE TIME OF THE SLAUGHTER.

AYIEEEEE!

AYIEEEEE!

IN THE MIDDLE OF ONE NIGHT, THOMPSON AND I WERE AWAKENED BY LOUD CRIES AND SHRIEKS OF LAMENTATION.

TATOOSCH'S SON HAD DIED.

AS MAQUINNA'S NEPHEW, THE BOY WAS CONSIDERED A TYEE AND SHOWN GREAT HONOR.

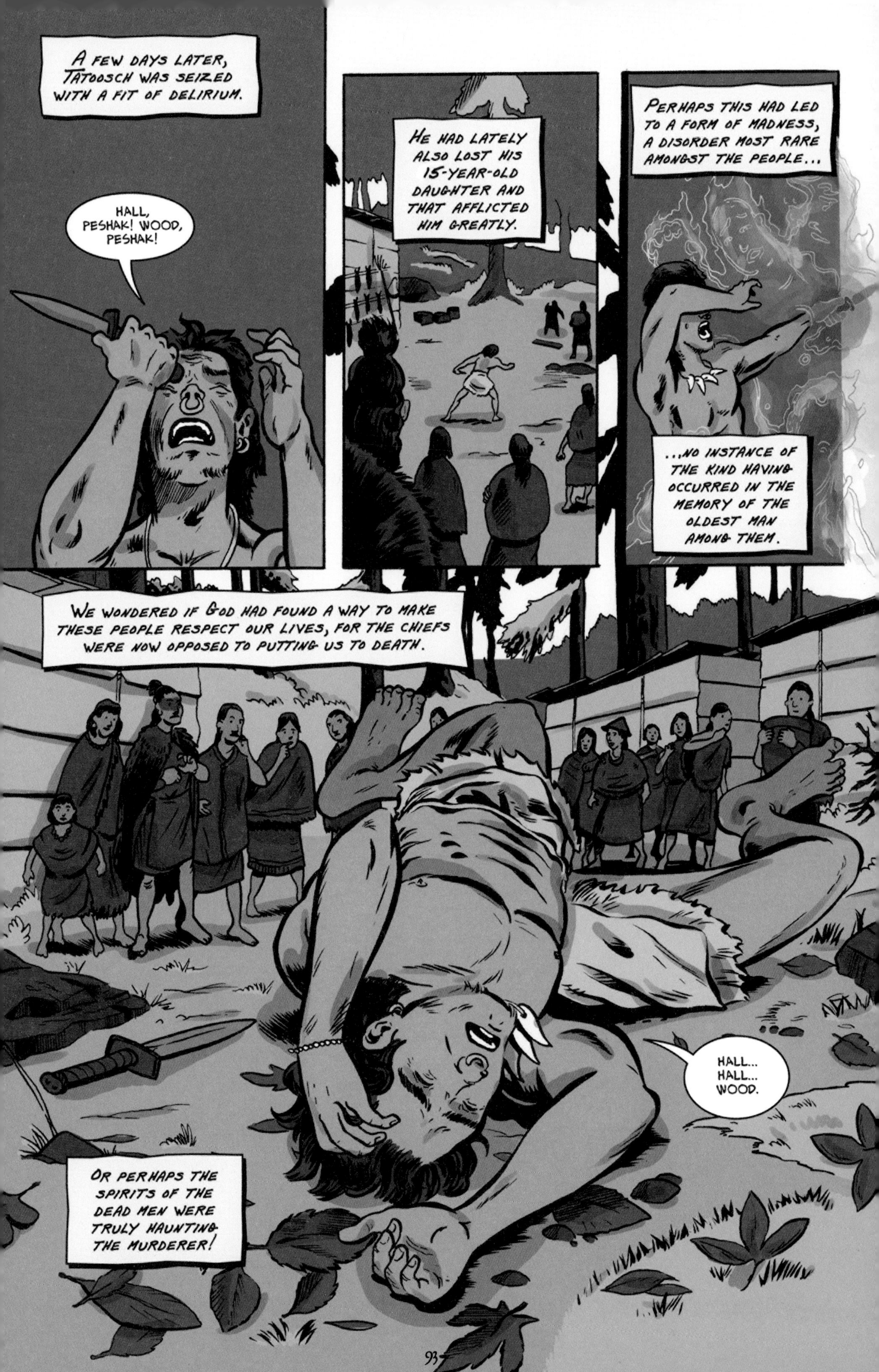
A FEW DAYS LATER, TATOOSCH WAS SEIZED WITH A FIT OF DELIRIUM.
HALL, PESHAK! WOOD, PESHAK!
HE HAD LATELY ALSO LOST HIS 15-YEAR-OLD DAUGHTER AND THAT AFFLICTED HIM GREATLY.
PERHAPS THIS HAD LED TO A FORM OF MADNESS, A DISORDER MOST RARE AMONGST THE PEOPLE...
...NO INSTANCE OF THE KIND HAVING OCCURRED IN THE MEMORY OF THE OLDEST MAN AMONG THEM.
WE WONDERED IF GOD HAD FOUND A WAY TO MAKE THESE PEOPLE RESPECT OUR LIVES, FOR THE CHIEFS WERE NOW OPPOSED TO PUTTING US TO DEATH.
HALL... HALL... WOOD.
OR PERHAPS THE SPIRITS OF THE DEAD MEN WERE TRULY HAUNTING THE MURDERER!

YOU MUST REST.

AND YOU MUST EAT.

PTHHHHH!

*TATOOSCH COULD THINK OF NOTHING OTHER THAN THE MEN HE HAD KILLED.*

WHAT TROUBLES YOU?

IT IS HALL. IT IS WOOD. THEY ARE HERE AND WILL NOT LEAVE ME ALONE!

JOHN, SPEAK TO HIM!

HALL AND WOOD ARE NOT HERE. ONLY WE ARE HERE.

I KNOW VERY WELL YOU DO NOT SEE THEM. BUT I DO!

I DO NOT SEE HALL OR WOOD EITHER.

HALL! WOOD! LEAVE ME IN PEACE!

WHAT DO YOU THINK IS WRONG WITH HIM?

SOMETHING IS INJURED IN HIS HEAD. HE SEES THINGS DIFFERENTLY NOW.

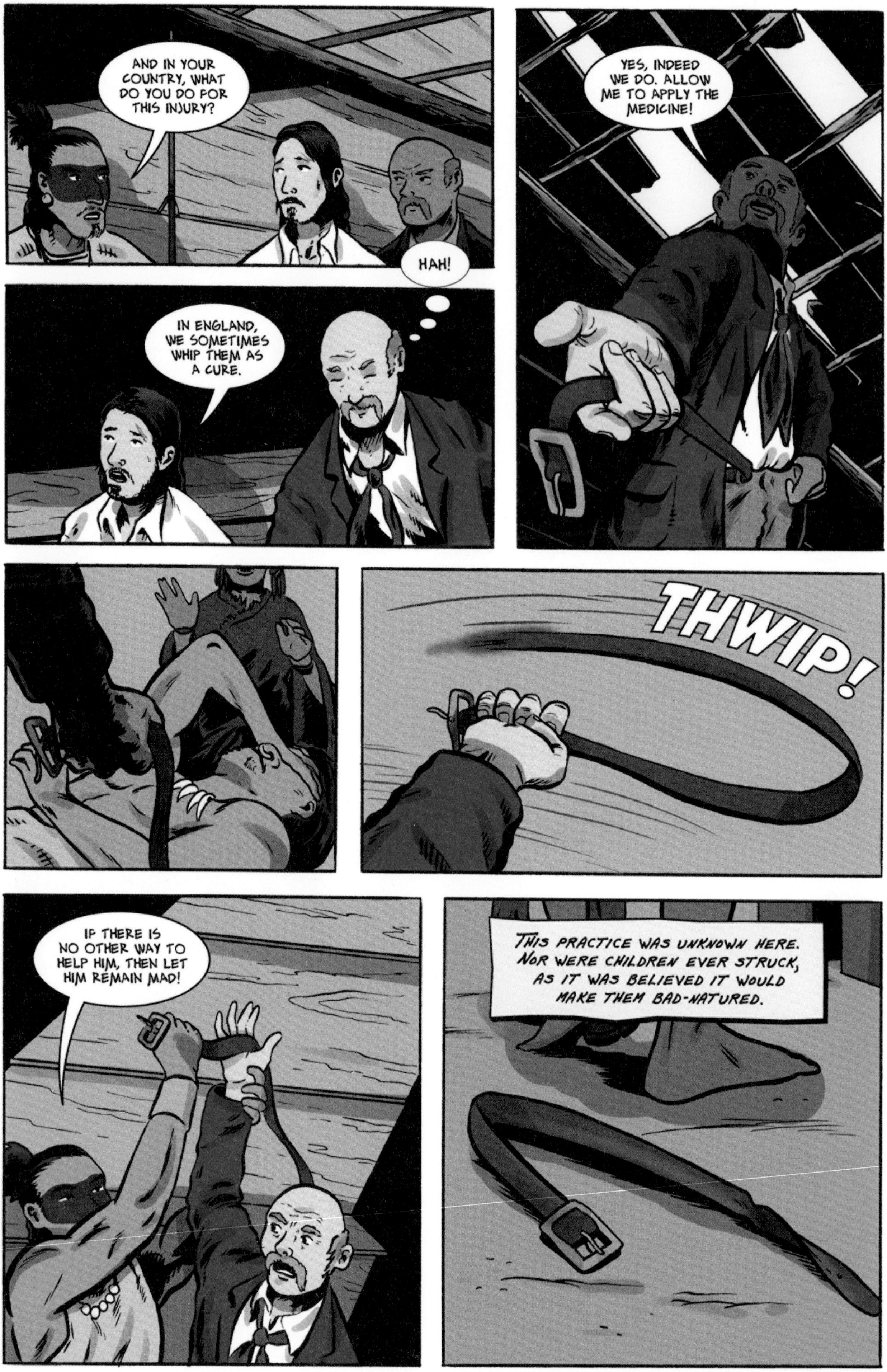
AND IN YOUR COUNTRY, WHAT DO YOU DO FOR THIS INJURY?
HAH!
YES, INDEED WE DO. ALLOW ME TO APPLY THE MEDICINE!
IN ENGLAND, WE SOMETIMES WHIP THEM AS A CURE.
THWIP!
IF THERE IS NO OTHER WAY TO HELP HIM, THEN LET HIM REMAIN MAD!
THIS PRACTICE WAS UNKNOWN HERE. NOR WERE CHILDREN EVER STRUCK, AS IT WAS BELIEVED IT WOULD MAKE THEM BAD-NATURED.

AS FOR TATOOSCH, OVER TIME HE BECAME STILL MORE DERANGED.

EVEN HIS WIFE FINALLY MOVED FROM HIS HOUSE TO MAQUINNA'S.

THE MAN WHO HAD SLAUGHTERED TWO OF MY MATES WOULD REMAIN HAUNTED FOR THE REST OF HIS DAYS.

# CHAPTER 8
## Hunter and Hunted

WITH SPRING, THE WHALING SEASON COMMENCED.

PPPSHH!

IN PREPARATION, MAQUINNA FASTED AND BATHED SEVERAL TIMES EACH DAY FOR MANY WEEKS...

...SEEKING THE AID OF HIS ANCESTOR-SPIRITS.

ONLY MAQUINNA'S NOBLES WERE PERMITTED TO JOIN THE HUNT. THEY TOO BATHED RITUALLY AND RUBBED THEIR BODIES AND FACES WITH SHELLS AND BRIARS.

THEY IMITATE THE WHALE...

...GETTING CLOSE TO ITS SPIRIT.

PFFF!

AND YET WITH ALL OF THIS, FOR QUITE SOME TIME MAQUINNA HAD NO SUCCESS FINDING A WHALE.

AND WHEN HE FINALLY SIGHTED ONE, HIS HARPOON SNAPPED.

KRAAAK!

ON ANOTHER OCCASION THE ROPE BROKE, AND FINALLY, THE MUSSEL-SHELL BLADE ITSELF SHATTERED.

SNAP!

PERHAPS I COULD FASHION A HARPOON THAT WOULD NOT FAIL YOU.

ANOTHER TIME OF GREAT HUNGER SOON SET IN. DAY AFTER DAY, THE MEN CAME BACK WITHOUT FISH IN A TIME WHEN THERE IS USUALLY PLENTY.

OUR HEALTH HAD BEEN GOOD THESE LAST THIRTEEN MONTHS.

BUT NOW A CRAMPING ACHE SEIZED MY STOMACH.

A HEAVY FLUX CAME UPON US, DUE TO THE POOR PROVISIONS WE NOW ATE. I FOUND MYSELF WEAK AND DESPERATELY ILL.

THE PEOPLE BLAME ME FOR THERE BEING NO FISH.

THEIR ANGER HAS TURNED AGAINST ME.

HERE IS A NEW HARPOON I HAVE FORGED FOR YOU. THIS ONE IS MADE OF STEEL.

THUS ARMED, MAQUINNA WENT TO SEA AGAIN. AND THIS TIME, HE WAS ABLE TO STRIKE RIGHT TO THE HEART.

SEALSKIN FLOATS ADDED DRAG, WHICH SLOWED THE WHALE DOWN AND KEPT HIM FROM DIVING.

BUT IT STILL TOOK MANY HOURS FOR THE MIGHTY CREATURE TO WEAKEN.

WHEN THE WHALE FINALLY DIED, A MAN SEWED THE HUGE MOUTH CLOSED LEST THE BEAST FILL WITH WATER AND SINK.

AND FINALLY THE HUNGRY PEOPLE KNEW THERE WOULD BE FOOD FOR THEIR STOMACHS.

WOCASH!

WOCASH TYEE!

BOK! BOK! BOK!

MAQUINNA HAD THE PRIVILEGE OF MAKING THE FIRST CUT...

... AND OF DIRECTING THE FIRST PADDLERS IN THE BUTCHERING AND DISTRIBUTION OF THE REST OF THE BLUBBER.

YOUR HARPOON WAS VERY GOOD, JOHN. YOU WILL SHARE IN THE BLUBBER, TOO.

IN CELEBRATION, ALL THE VILLAGERS WERE INVITED TO MAQUINNA'S HOME FOR A FEAST. BUT THE BEST PART OF THE WHALE — THE DORSAL FIN — WAS SET ASIDE AND GIVEN SPECIAL HONOR IN THANKS FOR ALLOWING ITSELF TO BE TAKEN.

IN EARLY JUNE, THE HAUNTED CHIEF, TATOOSCH, DIED.

WE ALL MADE OUR WAY A GOOD DISTANCE FROM THE VILLAGE FOR HIS BURIAL.

TATOOSCH'S FAMILY MEMBERS HAD CUT THEIR HAIR SHORT AS A TOKEN OF THEIR GRIEF.

YOU WILL SURELY MEET HIM AGAIN IN THE NEXT LIFETIME.

TATOOSCH'S MOST VALUABLE POSSESSIONS WERE BURIED WITH HIM.

NO, JOHN. THAT IS THE END OF HIM.

AND SO IT IS FOR ALL PEOPLE.

LATER, HIS OTHER POSSESSIONS WERE BURNED, WITH EXTRA OIL ADDED TO INCREASE THE FLAME.

TATOOSCH WAS HONORED WITH ANOTHER FEAST. BUT SOON THE FEASTING DAYS WOULD END.

THE GREAT HUNGER HAD RETURNED. AND SO HAD THE ANGER TOWARD MAQUINNA.

THE SALMON HAVE BEEN DRIVEN AWAY BY THE BLOOD OF THE BOSTON MEN.

IT IS MAQUINNA'S FAULT.

TRADERS NO LONGER COME SINCE MAQUINNA MURDERED THE BOSTON.

MAQUINNA GREW TO FEAR THE DISCONTENT.

YOU WILL BOTH GUARD ME, FROM NOW ON.

WHILE HE WAS THUS FAVORABLY DISPOSED TOWARD US, I TOLD HIM OF THE ILL TREATMENT WE OFTEN RECEIVED.

BUT MY CHIEF, YOUR OWN PEOPLE THROW ROCKS AT US. VISITING TRIBES INSULT US AS WELL.

THEN YOU SHALL REMAIN ARMED AT ALL TIMES.

AND I ALLOW YOU TO KILL ANYONE WHO ENDANGERS ME ...OR ABUSES YOU!

MAQUINNA'S PERMISSION WAS PUT TO THE TEST ONLY A FEW DAYS LATER AT THE POND WHERE WE WASHED OUR CLOTHING AND MAQUINNA'S BLANKETS.

NOW THE WHITE SLAVES WILL HAVE TO WORK FOR THEIR MASTER ALL DAY!

DO IT AGAIN AND I WILL KILL YOU!

THE MAN DID NOT KNOW THOMPSON'S TEMPER AS I DID.

SSSSSSSSSSWICK!

WITHOUT FURTHER WARNING, THOMPSON CUT OFF HIS HEAD!

WE BROUGHT THE FOOT-PRINTED BLANKET TO MAQUINNA...

...AND INFORMED HIM OF WHAT HAD TRANSPIRED.

FINALLY, THOMPSON'S BITTER AND ANGRY NATURE HAD EARNED HIM RESPECT.

THIS IS WELL DONE, TAMSIN. YOU HAVE THE MAKINGS OF A WARRIOR.

FROM THAT DAY FORWARD, THE PEOPLE TREATED US WITH HIGHER REGARD.

SOON YOU WILL SHOW ME HOW BRAVE YOU TRULY ARE.

THE BLOODSHED WAS JUST BEGINNING. MAQUINNA INFORMED US HE WAS PLANNING A RAID AND WE WOULD BE EXPECTED TO FIGHT ALONGSIDE HIS MEN.

# CHAPTER 9
## Love and Death in Nootka Sound

IT WAS A LATE SUMMER DAY WHEN MAQUINNA MADE HIS FEARSOME PRONOUNCEMENT.

THE A-Y-CHARTS LIVED ABOUT FIFTY MILES TO THE SOUTH. THERE HAD BEEN SOME CONTROVERSY WITH THEM THE PREVIOUS SUMMER.

WE ARE GOING TO FIGHT THE A-Y-CHARTS.

YOU WILL MAKE WEAPONS FOR MY WARRIORS.

BUT FOR ME ALONE, SOMETHING SPECIAL. SOMETHING THAT CAN KILL WITH A SINGLE BLOW TO THE HEAD.

I QUICKLY SET TO WORK AND FASHIONED WHAT HE REQUESTED, ADDING MY OWN EMBELLISHMENT.

THE TRIBE CONSISTED OF ABOUT 500 WARRIORS, MORE NUMEROUS THAN ANY OTHER TRIBE, AND ALSO POSSESSING GREATER STRENGTH AND COMBATIVE SPIRIT.

IN PREPARATION FOR WAR, FOR WEEKS THEY TOUGHENED THEIR SKIN BY SCRUBBING THEMSELVES WITH BUSHES MIXED WITH BRIARS.

AS THEY LACERATED THEMSELVES, THEY CHANTED TO THEIR GOD.

WOCASH QUAHOOTZE.

WOCASH QUAHOOTZE.

LET ME LIVE. NOT BE SICK.

FIND THE ENEMY. NOT FEAR HIM.

FIND HIM ASLEEP. KILL A GREAT MANY.

JOHN! TAMSIN!

YOU MUST PREPARE WITH US IN ORDER TO HARDEN YOUR SKIN AGAINST THE ENEMY'S WEAPONS.

WE DECLINED MAQUINNA'S ENTREATY.

ON THE CHOSEN EVENING, MAQUINNA TOSSED A BLACK SHINING POWDER CALLED PELPELTH ONTO HIS FACE, SO THAT IT GLITTERED FIERCELY.

BY MIDNIGHT WE CAME IN SIGHT OF THE VILLAGE, BUT WE WAITED MANY HOURS BEFORE MAKING OUR MOVE.

MAQUINNA COMMANDED HIS MEN TO ATTACK AT DAWN, WHEN THE ENEMY WOULD STILL BE ASLEEP.

WE FINALLY WENT AROUND THE VILLAGE SO WE COULD SURPRISE THE FOE FROM THE REAR.

WE MAINTAINED AN ABSOLUTE SILENCE.

AND THEN AT THE CHOSEN MOMENT, MAQUINNA SOUNDED HIS WAR CRY.

THE A-Y-CHART CHIEF, COMPLETELY SURPRISED, WAS UNABLE TO MOUNT RESISTANCE.

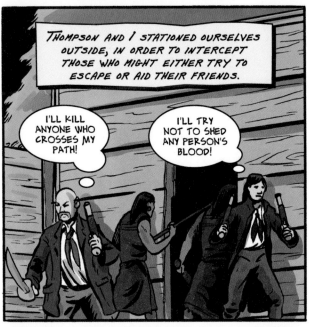

THOMPSON AND I STATIONED OURSELVES OUTSIDE, IN ORDER TO INTERCEPT THOSE WHO MIGHT EITHER TRY TO ESCAPE OR AID THEIR FRIENDS.

I'LL KILL ANYONE WHO CROSSES MY PATH!

I'LL TRY NOT TO SHED ANY PERSON'S BLOOD!

WE EACH ACHIEVED OUR DESIRED GOAL.

BY DAY'S END THOMPSON HAD KILLED SEVEN STOUT FELLOWS.

I MYSELF WAS SATISFIED TO SIMPLY TAKE SEVERAL MEN CAPTIVE.

WE DEPARTED WITH MANY CAPTIVES AND OTHER SPOILS OF OUR VICTORY...

...AND WERE WELCOMED HOME TO THE PEOPLE'S JOYFUL DRUMMING.

I CONGRATULATE YOU, MY HUSBAND!

THOMPSON'S EXPLOITS EARNED HIM GREAT CREDIT. HE HAD JUST TURNED FORTY YEARS OLD.

WE WILL NAME YOU CHEHIEL-SUMA-HAR, AFTER OUR FAMOUS WARRIOR.

AND YOU, JOHN, YOU TOOK FOUR CAPTIVES. I WILL ALLOW THEM TO WORK FOR YOU.

I AM GRATEFUL TO YOU, MY CHIEF.

BUT HE WOULD SOON OFFER ME ANOTHER, FAR LESS WELCOME, REWARD.

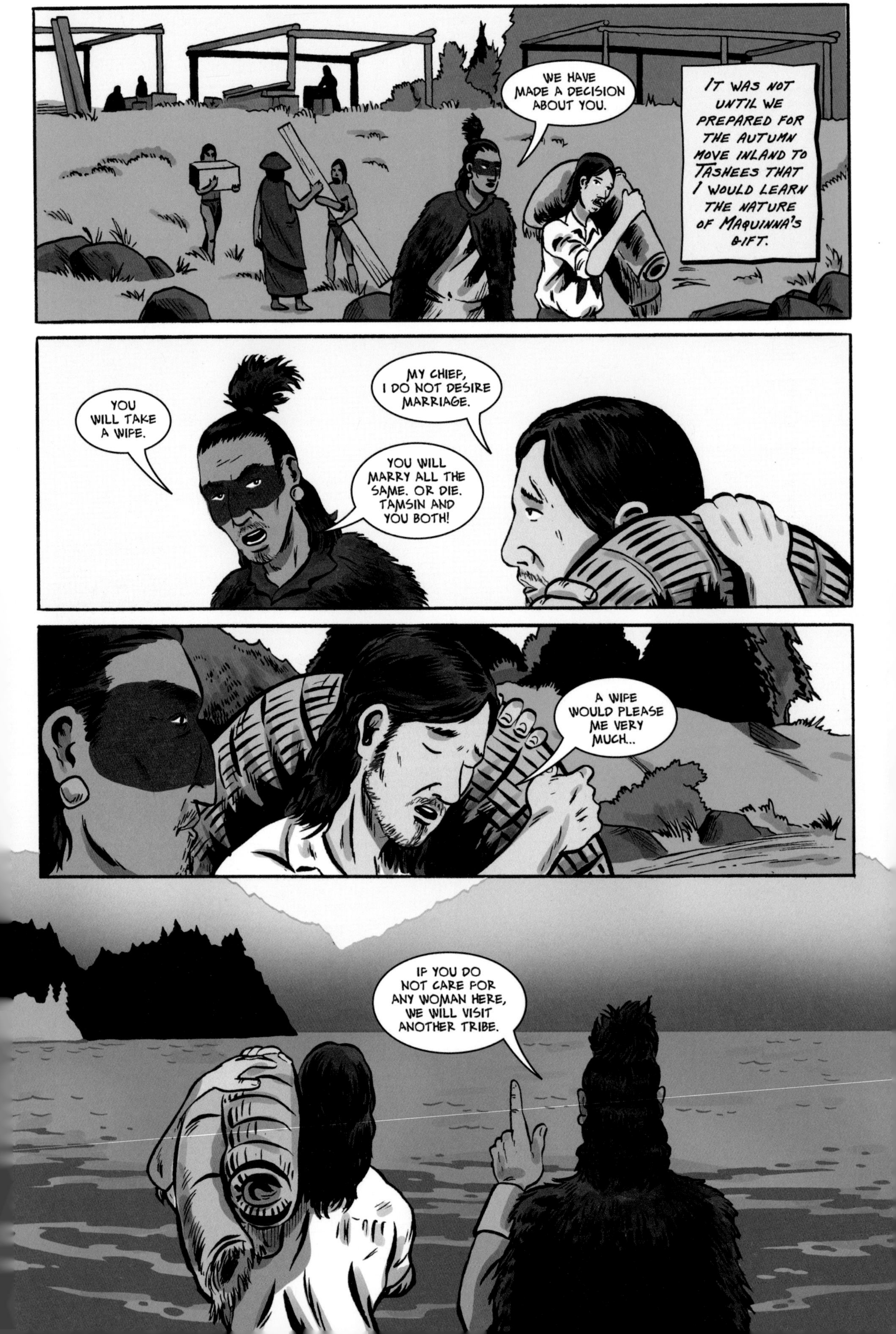
It was not until we prepared for the autumn move inland to Tashees that I would learn the nature of Maquinna's gift.
We have made a decision about you.
You will take a wife.
My chief, I do not desire marriage.
You will marry all the same. Or die. Tamsin and you both!
A wife would please me very much...
If you do not care for any woman here, we will visit another tribe.

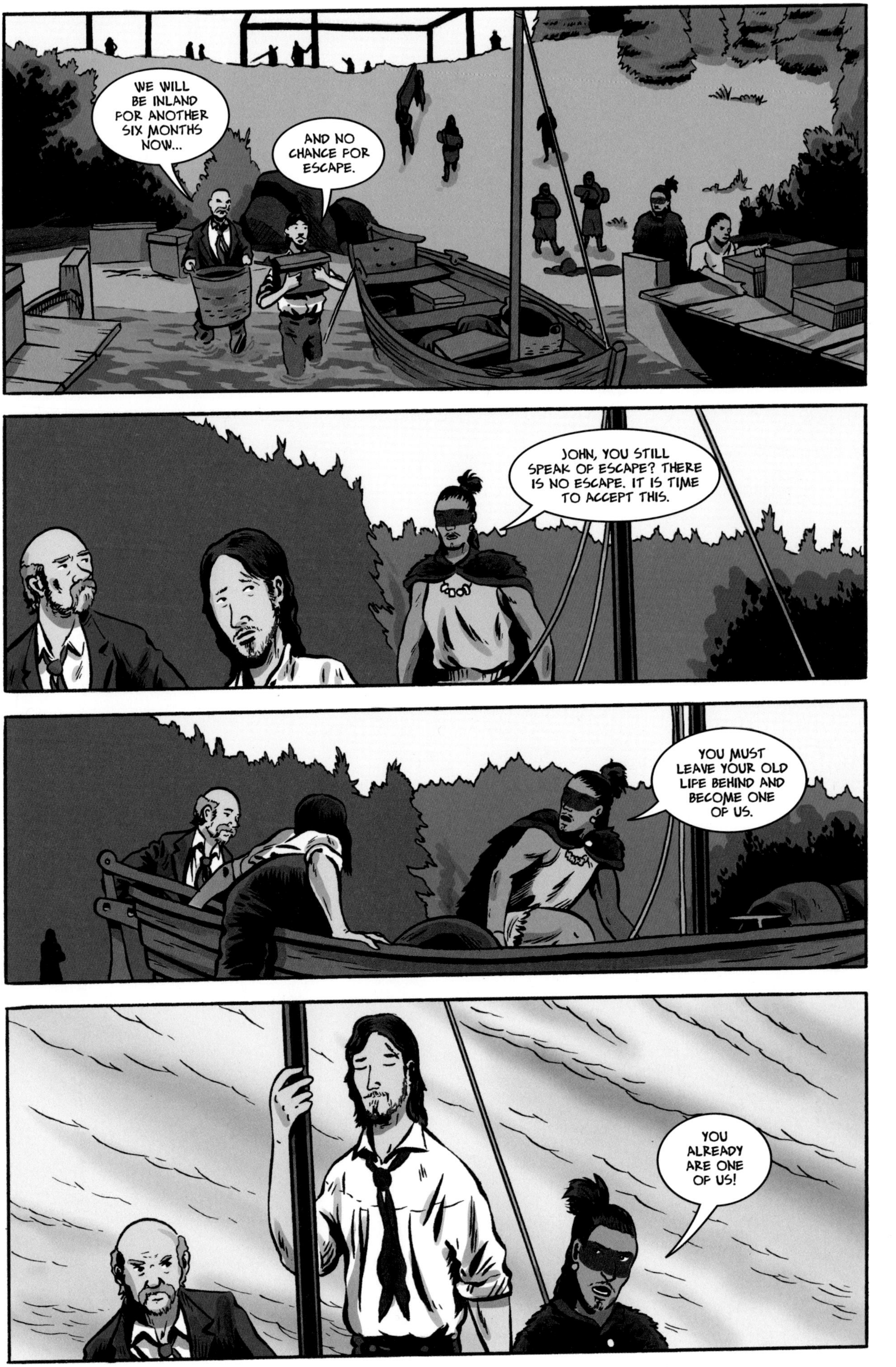
WE WILL BE INLAND FOR ANOTHER SIX MONTHS NOW...
AND NO CHANCE FOR ESCAPE.
JOHN, YOU STILL SPEAK OF ESCAPE? THERE IS NO ESCAPE. IT IS TIME TO ACCEPT THIS.
YOU MUST LEAVE YOUR OLD LIFE BEHIND AND BECOME ONE OF US.
YOU ALREADY ARE ONE OF US!

WELL AFTER WE HAD SETTLED INTO *TASHEES*, MAQUINNA AGAIN RAISED THE DREADED SUBJECT.

A WIFE WILL MAKE YOU MORE CONTENTED HERE.

TODAY WE WILL RETURN TO THE AI-TIZ-ZART TO FIND YOUR MATE.

TODAY?!

IT WAS STILL VERY MUCH AGAINST MY INCLINATION TO TAKE A NATIVE WOMAN AS A PARTNER. BUT MAQUINNA WOULD NOT BE DISSUADED.

WITH THE AID OF OUR PADDLES, SAILS, AND A FAIR BREEZE, WE ARRIVED AT *AI-TIZ-ZART* BEFORE SUNSET. I NOW UNDERSTOOD WHY WE HAD VISITED ONCE BEFORE.

We were again warmly welcomed, this time with a feast of herring spawn.

Is there any woman here you might consider for marriage?

There was one girl I had noticed on our last visit. She would have been considered lovely in any country.

Who is that over there?

She is Eu-stoch-ee-exqua, the daughter of Chief Upquesta.

MAQUINNA WASTED NO TIME.

COME WITH ME.

HE ORDERED HIS MEN TO RETURN WITH BOXES OF GIFTS WE HAD BROUGHT WITH US.

YOU HAVE ONCE BEFORE MET JOHN, WHO REMINDS YOU OF A SEAL.

AH, THE ONE WHO NEEDS A MATE.

JOHN FAVORS YOUR DAUGHTER.

HE IS VERY VALUABLE AND CAN MAKE EXCELLENT DAGGERS AND HARPOONS.

AH, BUT SHE IS MY ONLY DAUGHTER AND IS VERY VALUABLE TO ME.

JOHN HAS A GOOD TEMPER AND IS LOVED BY ALL THE PEOPLE—EVEN THE CHILDREN.

AS I LOVE MY DAUGHTER, I COULD NOT THINK OF PARTING WITH HER.

WE HAVE BROUGHT MUCH CLOTH, MANY MUSKETS, AND EXCELLENT SEA OTTER SKINS WITH US.

WELL, THEN. COME HERE, MY CHILD. MEET JOHN.

IF SHE ACCEPTS YOU, YOU MUST PROMISE TO TAKE VERY GOOD CARE OF MY DAUGHTER.

THE CHIEF CONCLUDED BY CONSENTING TO THE PROPOSED UNION. AND SO DID EU-STOCH-EE-EXQUA.

MEN, RETURN THESE PRESENTS TO JOHN, AND TWO SLAVES AS WELL, TO HELP HIM FISH...

...IT IS SAID THIS IS NOT HIS GREATEST SKILL!

WE SOON DEPARTED, BUT THE WIND WAS NOT WITH US FOR THE RETURN TO TASHEES.

IT WAS VERY EARLY THE NEXT MORNING BEFORE WE ARRIVED. THAT WAS WHEN I LEARNED THE MEANING OF MY BRIDE'S NAME: SUNRISE.

# CHAPTER 10
## For Better or Worse

SOON AFTER OUR RETURN HOME, WE CELEBRATED MY MARRIAGE. I WOULD NOW HAVE A COMPANION WITH WHOM TO SHARE THE COLD NIGHTS THAT LAY AHEAD.

I AM GLAD YOU HAVE CHOSEN ME, JOHN.

YOU WILL LIVE HERE, BETWEEN MY BROTHER AND ME.

I WANT TO LIVE WITH CWAN, TOO!

THERE HAD BEEN MUCH JOY AT MY WEDDING. BUT MY OWN FEELINGS WERE CONFUSED.

I NOW HAD A HOME OF MY OWN...

A MATE OF MY OWN...

THIS WILL BE MORE COMFORTABLE THAN SLEEPING ON THE FLOOR.

I PROMISE NO ONE WILL PULL YOUR PANTS DOWN AGAIN!

IN FACT, A FAMILY OF MY OWN.

HUSBAND, IT IS TIME FOR SLEEP.

AND YET I FELT UNEASY.

I FOUND MY BRIDE BOTH AMIABLE AND INTELLIGENT. I KNEW I SHOULD BE HAPPY WITH SUCH A WIFE.

BUT TO ME, THIS FORCED MARRIAGE WAS A CHAIN THAT WOULD BIND ME FOREVER TO THIS WILD LAND.

NONETHELESS, I TOOK GREAT PAINS TO KEEP MY FAMILY NEAT, CLEAN, AND FREE OF VERMIN.

MY CHIEFS HAVE MADE ANOTHER DECISION ABOUT YOU.

NOW THAT YOU HAVE MARRIED ONE OF OUR WOMEN, YOU WILL DRESS LIKE US.

YOU AND TAMSIN WILL WEAR THE KUTSAK. SOMETIMES YOU WILL WEAR NOTHING AT ALL.

MY CHIEF, WE CANNOT BEAR THE COLD AS THE NOOTKA PEOPLE DO.

YOU NO SAY NO!

THIS ORDER WAS TO ME MOST PAINFUL. IT SEEMED THAT WITH EACH DAY I GREW MORE REMOTE FROM THE ENGLISHMAN I HAD ONCE BEEN.

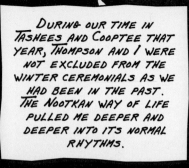

DURING OUR TIME IN TASHEES AND COOPTEE THAT YEAR, THOMPSON AND I WERE NOT EXCLUDED FROM THE WINTER CEREMONIALS AS WE HAD BEEN IN THE PAST. THE NOOTKAN WAY OF LIFE PULLED ME DEEPER AND DEEPER INTO ITS NORMAL RHYTHMS.

CWAN. CWAN. YOU MUST COME. QUICKLY!

BUT SOMETIMES, THE UNEXPECTED HAPPENED TOO.

IT WAS THE MIDDLE OF THE NIGHT IN JANUARY OF 1805...

SKY CODFISH WANTS TO SWALLOW THE MOON!

SKY CODFISH WAS A SUPERNATURAL CREATURE.

BOK! BOK! BOK!

BUT WE WILL DRIVE HIM AWAY!

AT LEAST THAT WAS WHAT THE PEOPLE BELIEVED THE LUNAR ECLIPSE TO BE.

BUT THE FIRES, DRUMMING, AND SINGING OF SPIRIT SONGS SOON FREED THE MOON FROM BEING DEVOURED. THE PEOPLE CLAIMED IT NEVER FAILED.

BOK! BOK! BOK!

124

I AM COLD. ALWAYS SO COLD.

COME INSIDE, HUSBAND.

IN SOME WAYS, MARRIAGE MADE LIFE MORE COMFORTABLE.

LET ME HELP WARM YOU!

BUT I STILL SUFFERED.

IF THE CHIEF WOULD ONLY ALLOW IT, THOMPSON COULD MAKE A JACKET AND TROUSERS FOR EACH OF US.

UNGHHH!

WHUMP!

AND THOMPSON SUFFERED EVEN MORE GREATLY.

WHAT IS WRONG?

THOMPSON HAD ALWAYS BEEN SO STRONG.

BUT NOW HE WAS FELLED BY RHEUMATISM.

FOR WEEKS, HE WAS TOO ILL TO GO OUTDOORS.

I WAS OBLIGED TO DO THE LABOR FOR US BOTH.

MY OWN LIFE BEGAN TO FEEL INTOLERABLE TO ME, AND I COULD FEEL MY DESIRE TO LIVE SLIP GRADUALLY AWAY.

STILL, I NEVER LOST MY RELIGIOUS FAITH.

WITH MAQUINNA'S PERMISSION, I RETIRED TO A SMALL LAKE NEARBY TO WORSHIP AND PRAY EVERY SUNDAY I WAS ABLE.

WHEN WE FINALLY RETURNED TO OUR QUARTERS AT NOOTKA, MY SENSATIONS WERE FAR DIFFERENT FROM THAT OF OUR LAST, HAPPIER RETURN.

THOMPSON HAD RECOVERED. BUT NOW, IT WAS I WHO FELL ILL.

JOHN! WHAT IS WRONG?

THE COLD OF THE WINTER AND THE LACK OF WARM CLOTHING HAD WEAKENED MY BODY AND MY SOUL.

CAN YOU STAND?

I FINALLY BELIEVE A SHIP WILL NEVER COME TO RELEASE US. WE SHALL NEVER LEAVE!

A FEW WEEKS LATER, I WAS TAKEN EVEN MORE ILL WITH A VIOLENT COLIC WHILE MAKING LANCES FOR THE COMING WHALE-HUNT SEASON.

THROUGHOUT MANY HOURS OF GREAT PAIN THERE WAS NOTHING COMFORTING TO TAKE, NOR ANYTHING TO DRINK BUT COLD WATER.

IT SEEMED AS IF I MIGHT DIE RIGHT THEN.

AND THE FOLLOWING DAY, ONE OF MAQUINNA'S SLAVES DID DIE.

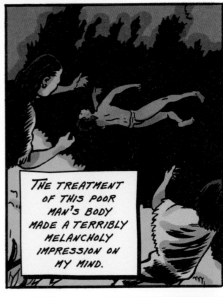

THE TREATMENT OF THIS POOR MAN'S BODY MADE A TERRIBLY MELANCHOLY IMPRESSION ON MY MIND.

I COULD NOT BUT THINK THAT IF I WERE TO DIE HERE...

...SUCH WOULD BE MY FATE AS WELL, A DEATH WITHOUT EVEN THE PRIVILEGE OF HAVING A LITTLE EARTH THROWN OVER MY REMAINS!

MY WIFE EMPLOYED THE NOOTKAN REMEDY FOR COLIC, BY RUBBING MY BELLY STRONGLY AND THEN WRAPPING ME TIGHTLY IN BEARSKIN IN ORDER TO PRODUCE PERSPIRATION.

EU-STOCH-EE-EXQUA, PLEASE DON'T LET CWAN DIE.

BOTH THE FEEBLENESS CAUSED BY MY ILLNESS AND MY SENSE OF HOPELESSNESS KEPT ME VERY MUCH INDISPOSED.

I WISH TO SPEAK WITH JOHN. ALONE.

NOW, JOHN. YOU WILL ANSWER YOUR CHIEF.

ARE YOU UNHAPPY WITH YOUR WIFE?

IS THAT THE CAUSE OF YOUR SADNESS?

IF THAT IS SO, I WILL ALLOW YOU TO PART WITH HER.

I CONSIDERED MY NEW WIFE; HER KINDNESS, HER MILDNESS, AND HER GENTLE DEVOTION TO ME.

IT IS I WHO SHOULD CARE FOR YOU. YET I CANNOT. I DO NOT THINK I WILL LIVE LONG.

NO! I MUST STAY WITH JOHN AND CARE FOR HIM.

YOU SHOULD GO HOME TO YOUR PEOPLE.

GO, SUNRISE, RETURN TO YOUR FATHER.

I DID NOT KNOW IT THEN, BUT SUNRISE WAS ALREADY WITH CHILD.

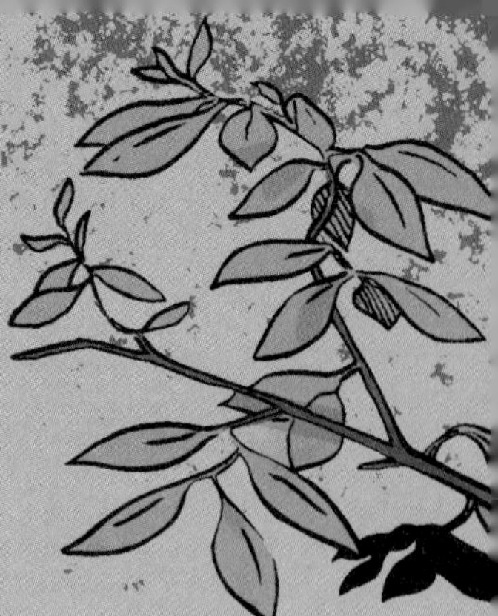

# CHAPTER II
## Final Lies

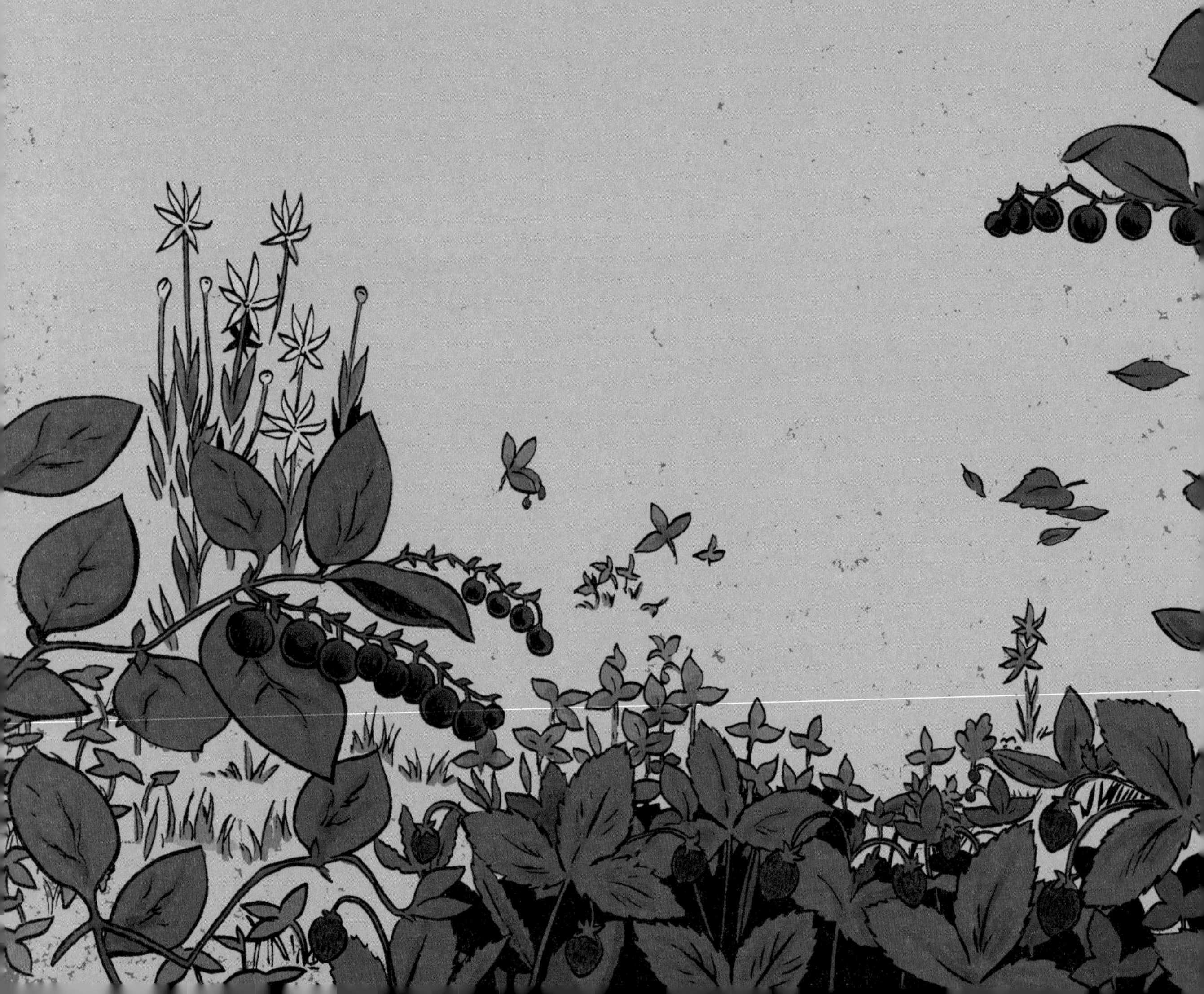

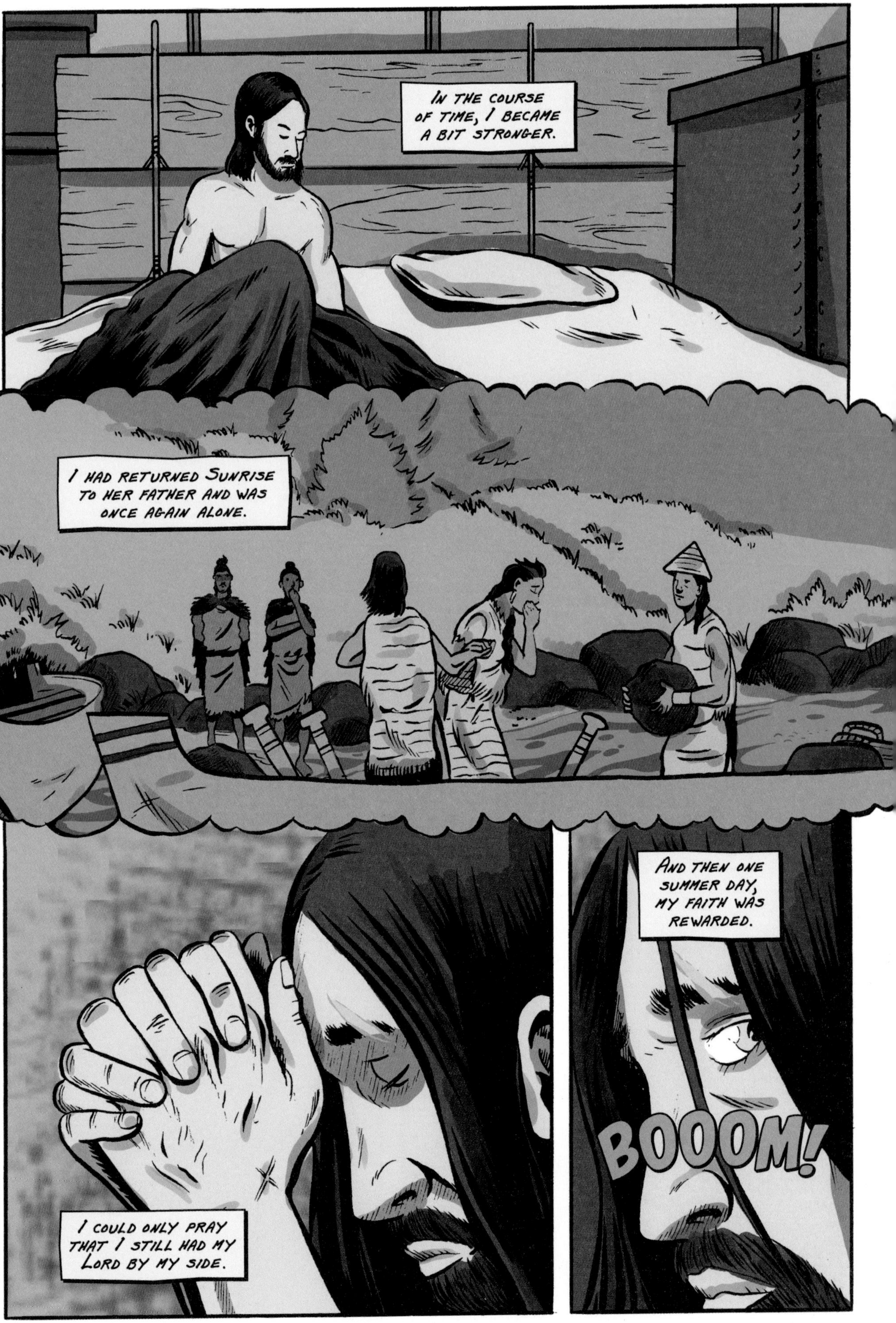
IN THE COURSE OF TIME, I BECAME A BIT STRONGER.
I HAD RETURNED SUNRISE TO HER FATHER AND WAS ONCE AGAIN ALONE.
I COULD ONLY PRAY THAT I STILL HAD MY LORD BY MY SIDE.
AND THEN ONE SUMMER DAY, MY FAITH WAS REWARDED.
BOOOM!

ON JULY 19, 1805, MY EARS WERE SALUTED BY THE SOUND OF THREE CANNON — THE TRADITIONAL SIGNAL OF A SHIP DESIRING TRADE.

BOOOM!

BOOOM!

WEENA, WEENA!*

WEENA, WEENA!*

MAMETHLEE!

MAMETHLEE!

*STRANGERS

MY HEART BOUNDED WITH JOY...

...BUT I PRETENDED TO PAY NO ATTENTION TO WHAT WAS BEING SAID.

DO NOT BETRAY ANY EMOTION AT ALL.

DO YOU NOT KNOW ABOUT THE APPROACHING SHIP?

IT MEANS NOTHING TO ME. I AM USED TO LIFE HERE NOW.

MAQUINNA REQUIRED THAT I JOIN A VILLAGE MEETING REGARDING THE SITUATION.

THE WHITE MEN ARE NEAR.

I ASK WHAT WE OUGHT TO DO ABOUT JOHN AND TAMSIN.

SEND THEM DEEP INTO THE COUNTRYSIDE UNTIL THE VESSEL DEPARTS!

AND SAY THAT ANOTHER NATION MURDERED THE BOSTON.

IT WAS THE KINDHEARTED TOOWINNAKINNISH WHO DEFENDED US.

JOHN HAS BEEN ILL. JOHN IS UNHAPPY.

LET US RETURN HIM AND HIS FATHER TO THE MAMETHLEE.

IT IS TRUE THAT I WISH TO TRADE.

BUT THE DANGER MIGHT BE TOO GREAT. JOHN, YOU SPEAK.

JOHN HAS ALWAYS BEEN TRUE.

*I BEGAN TO SEE THE CHANCE OF RESCUE, THOUGH IT WOULD REQUIRE MUCH DECEPTION.*

YOU HAVE NOTHING TO FEAR.

*MAQUINNA ASKED ME TO WRITE A LETTER TO THE CAPTAIN SAYING HOW WELL AND KINDLY I HAD BEEN TREATED.*

YES, JOHN, YOU WHO LIKE TO WRITE SO MUCH

YOU WILL DO THIS FOR YOUR CHIEF.

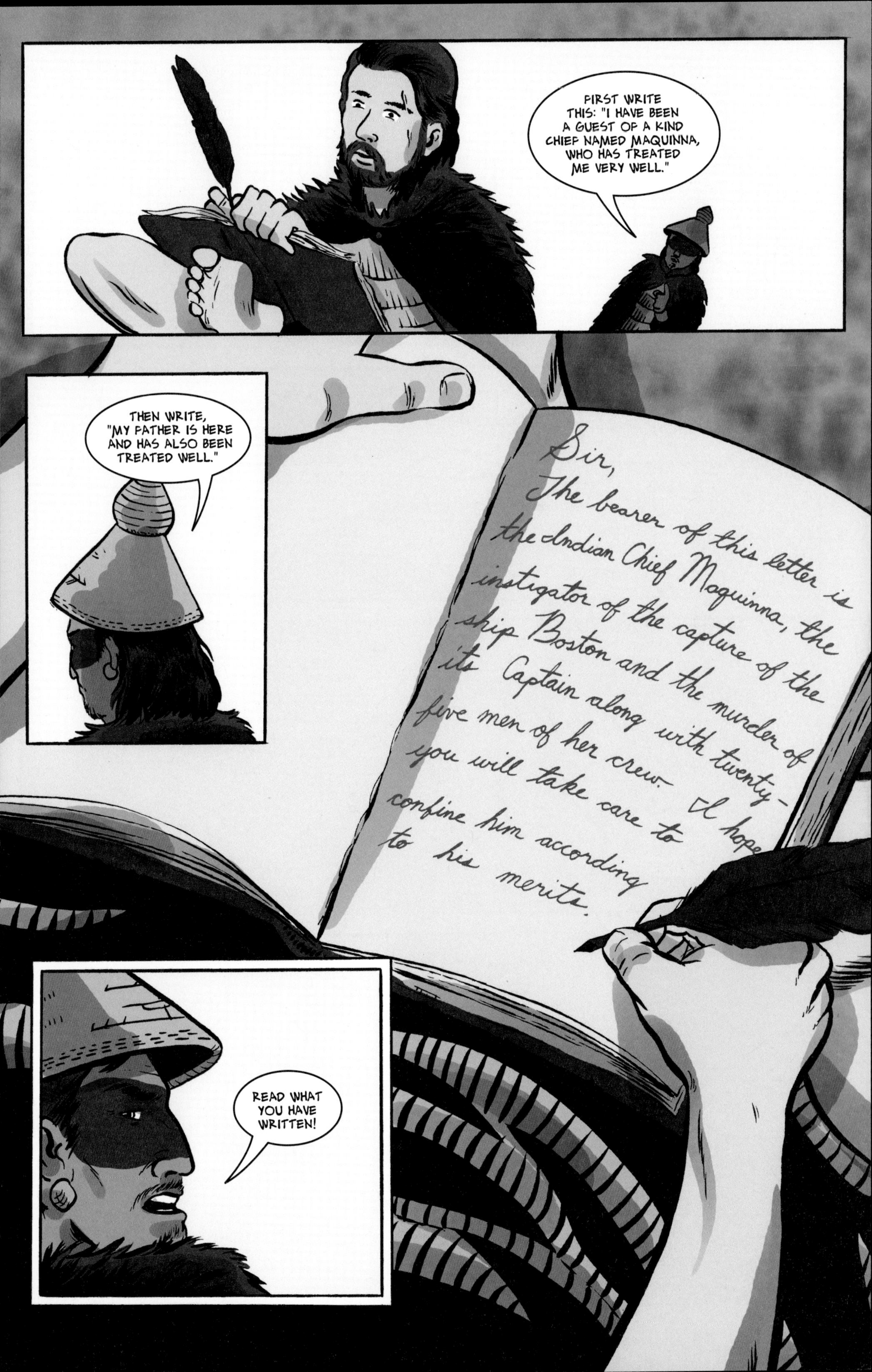
FIRST WRITE THIS: "I HAVE BEEN A GUEST OF A KIND CHIEF NAMED MAQUINNA, WHO HAS TREATED ME VERY WELL."
THEN WRITE, "MY FATHER IS HERE AND HAS ALSO BEEN TREATED WELL."
Sir,
The bearer of this letter is the Indian Chief Maquinna, the instigator of the capture of the ship Boston and the murder of its Captain along with twenty-five men of her crew. I hope you will take care to confine him according to his merits.
READ WHAT YOU HAVE WRITTEN!

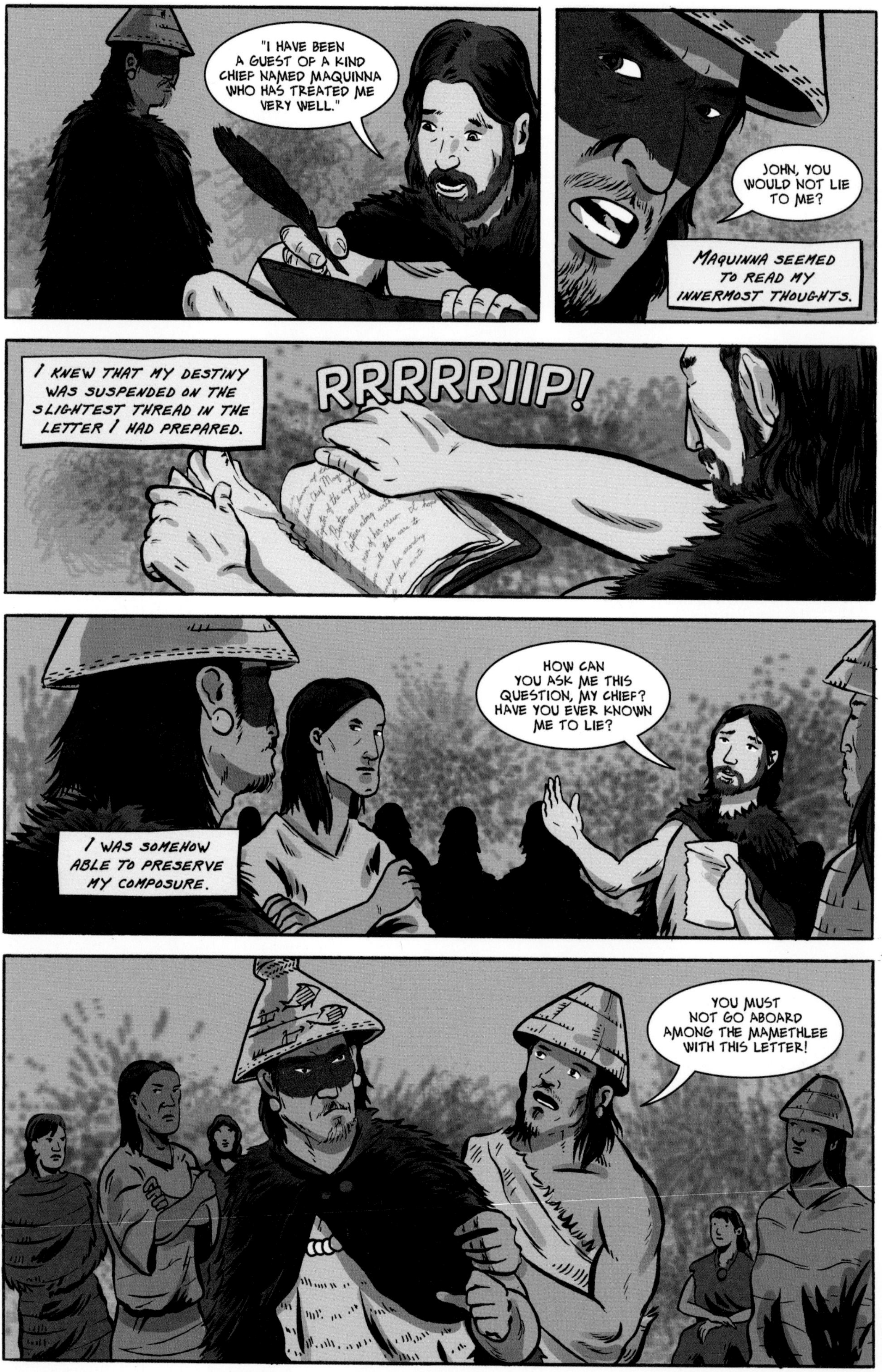
"I HAVE BEEN A GUEST OF A KIND CHIEF NAMED MAQUINNA WHO HAS TREATED ME VERY WELL."
JOHN, YOU WOULD NOT LIE TO ME?
MAQUINNA SEEMED TO READ MY INNERMOST THOUGHTS.
I KNEW THAT MY DESTINY WAS SUSPENDED ON THE SLIGHTEST THREAD IN THE LETTER I HAD PREPARED.
RRRRRIIP!
HOW CAN YOU ASK ME THIS QUESTION, MY CHIEF? HAVE YOU EVER KNOWN ME TO LIE?
I WAS SOMEHOW ABLE TO PRESERVE MY COMPOSURE.
YOU MUST NOT GO ABOARD AMONG THE MAMETHLEE WITH THIS LETTER!

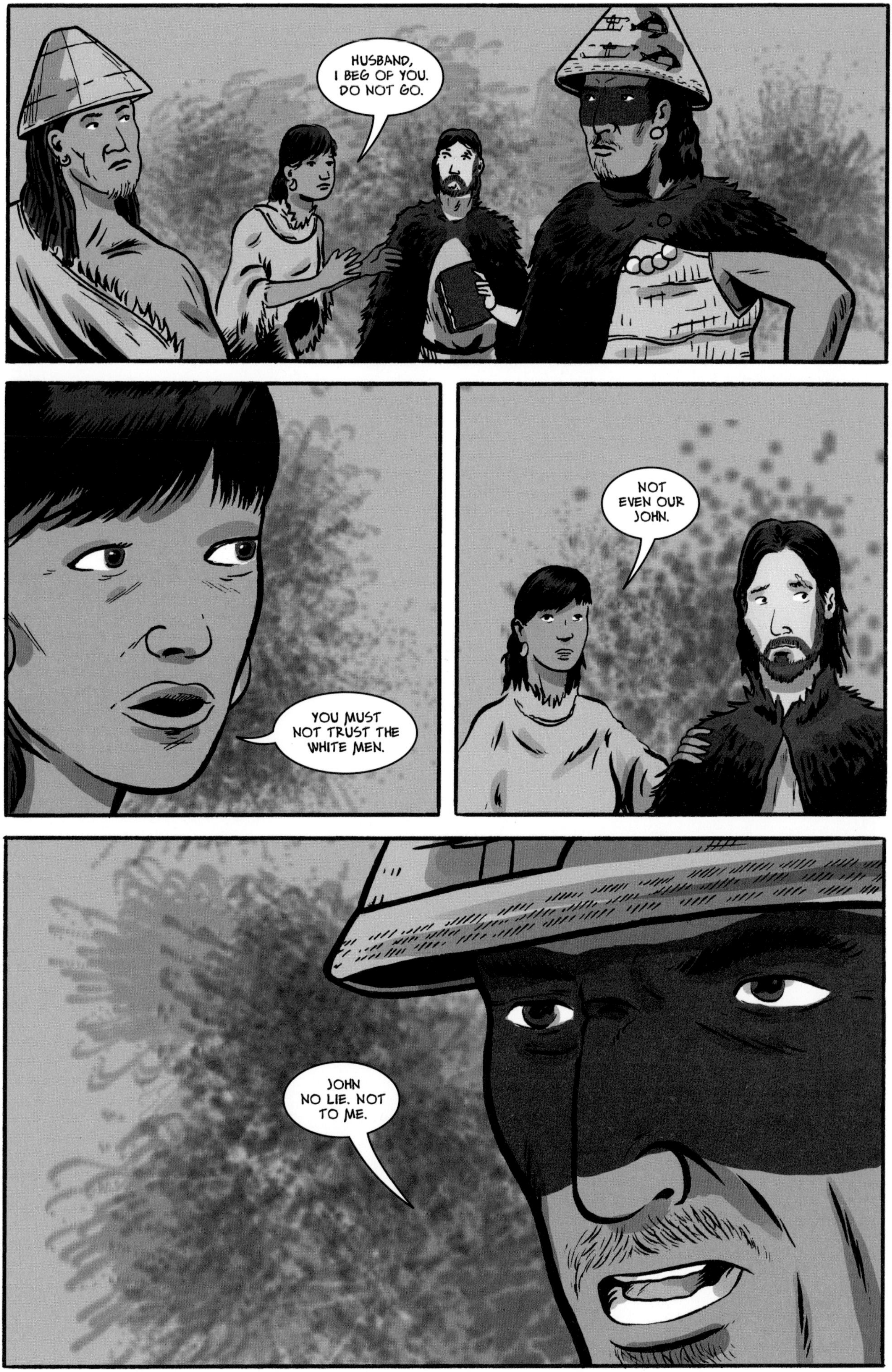
HUSBAND, I BEG OF YOU. DO NOT GO.
YOU MUST NOT TRUST THE WHITE MEN.
NOT EVEN OUR JOHN.
JOHN NO LIE. NOT TO ME.

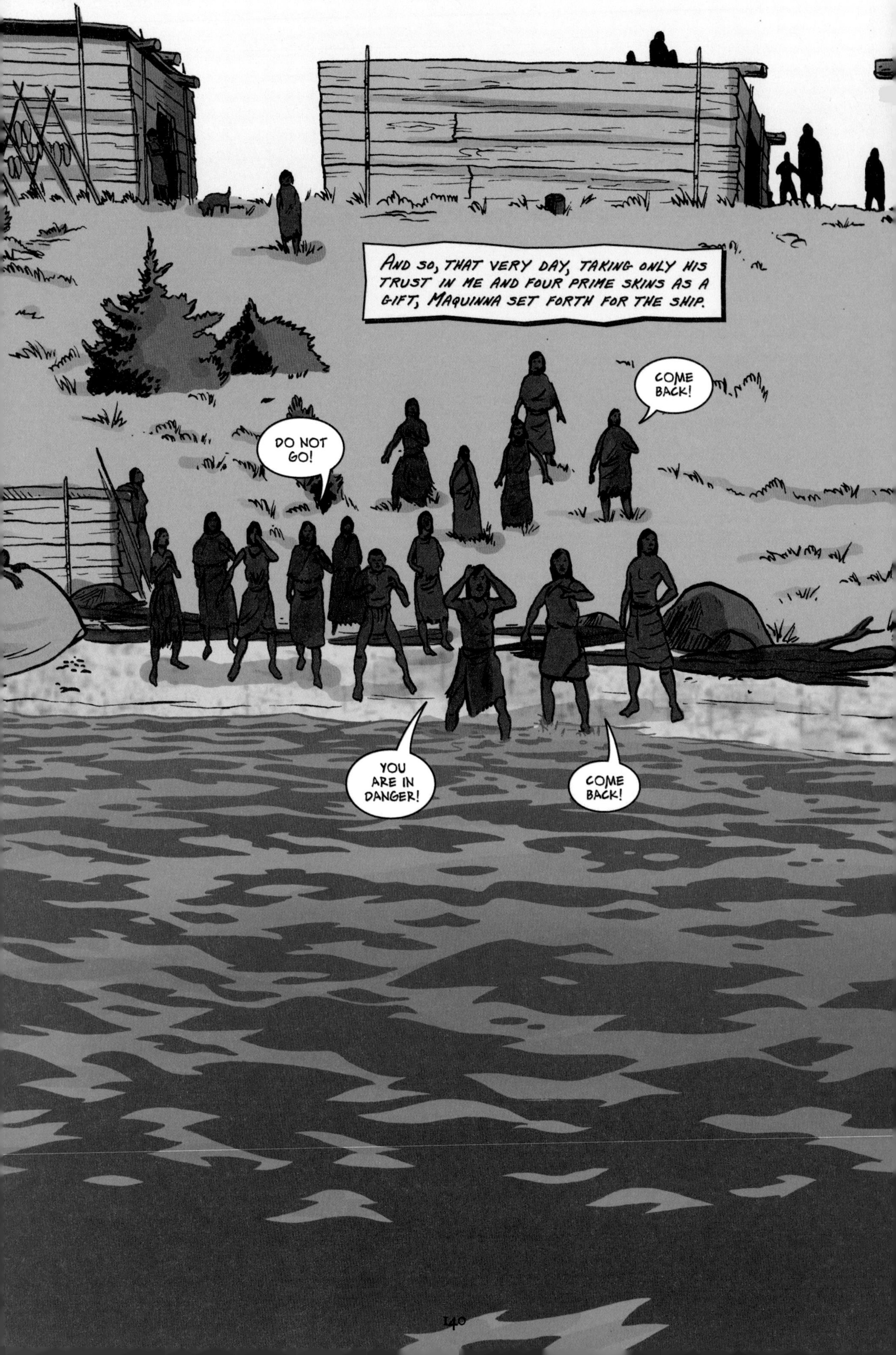
AND SO, THAT VERY DAY, TAKING ONLY HIS TRUST IN ME AND FOUR PRIME SKINS AS A GIFT, MAQUINNA SET FORTH FOR THE SHIP.
COME BACK!
DO NOT GO!
YOU ARE IN DANGER!
COME BACK!

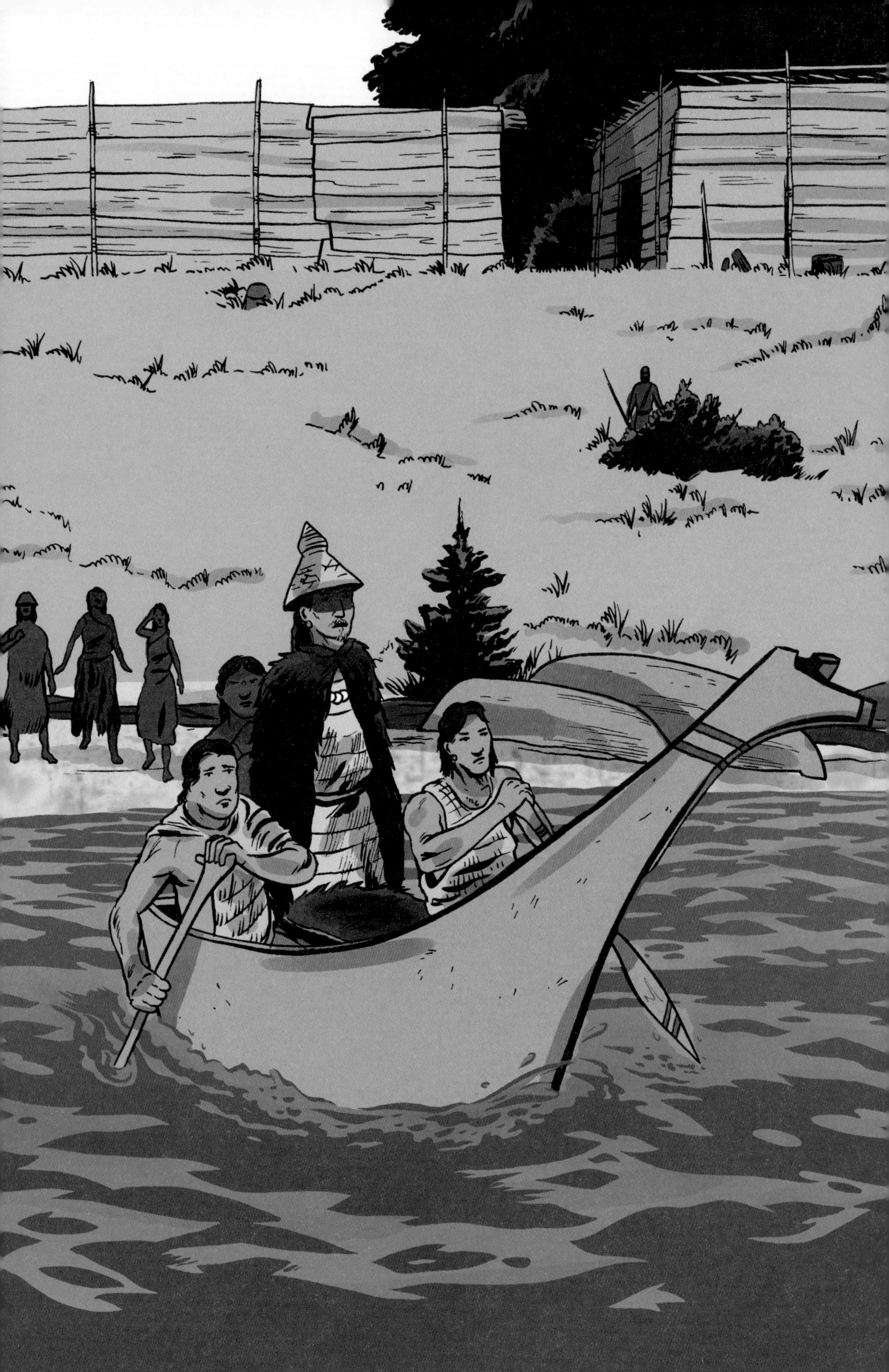

# CHAPTER 12
## That Desperate Shore

YOU ARE MOST WELCOME HERE, CHIEF!

I HAVE BROUGHT YOU FINE OTTER SKINS AS A PRESENT.

AND ALSO THIS LETTER TO INTRODUCE ME.

MAY I INVITE YOU TO MY CABIN FOR SOME RUM?

BUT EVEN AS HIS BEHAVIOR TOWARD THE CHIEF WAS CORDIAL, THE CAPTAIN, SAMUEL HILL, HAD PRIVATELY SIGNALED HIS MATE TO RETURN WITH A GROUP OF ARMED MEN.

AND PLEASE ENJOY SOME BISCUITS.

Whump!

YOU, SIR, ARE MY PRISONER!

AND SO YOU SHALL REMAIN...

...UNTIL BOTH SAILORS YOU HAVE TAKEN ARE RELEASED.

RUN, MEN, RUN!

SPLASH!

WHERE IS THE CHIEF?!

WHAT HAS HAPPENED?!

IT IS JOHN'S FAULT, HE SPOKE BAD ABOUT THE CHIEF!

HIS LETTER WAS A LIE!

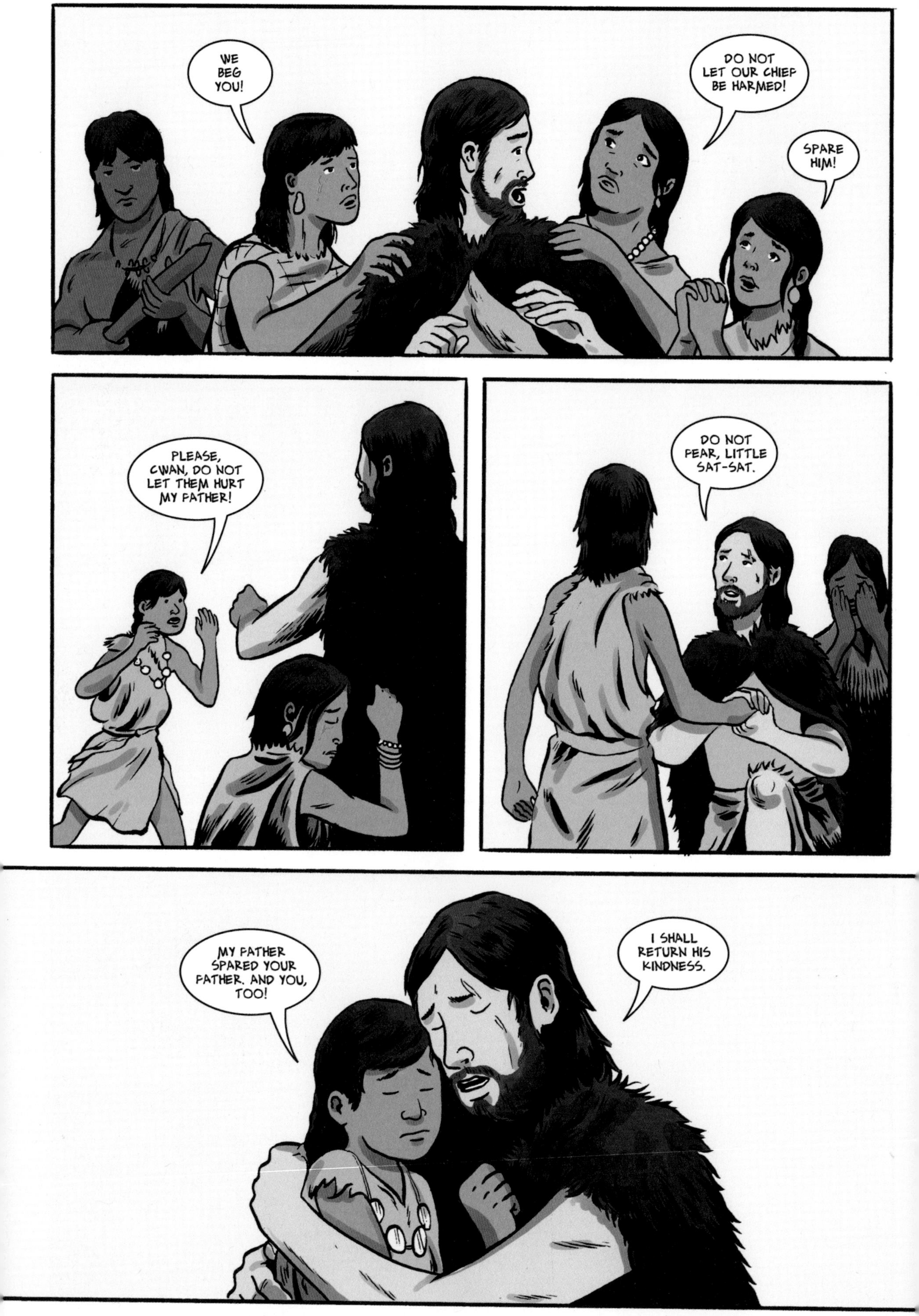
WE BEG YOU!
DO NOT LET OUR CHIEF BE HARMED!
SPARE HIM!
PLEASE, CWAN, DO NOT LET THEM HURT MY FATHER!
DO NOT FEAR, LITTLE SAT-SAT.
MY FATHER SPARED YOUR FATHER. AND YOU, TOO!
I SHALL RETURN HIS KINDNESS.

CUT JOHN INTO LITTLE PIECES!

BURN HIM OVER A SLOW FIRE...

...SUSPENDED BY HIS HEELS!

SILENCE! LET JOHN SPEAK.

KILL ME IF YOU WISH. BUT THE CAPTAIN KNOWS I AM HERE, AND IF YOU DO IT, YOU WILL IMMEDIATELY SEE YOUR CHIEF HANGING FROM THE YARDARM OF THE BRIG.

*AFTER MUCH DISCUSSION, THE PEOPLE AND I DEVISED A PLAN.*

IF YOU WISH TO SAVE YOUR CHIEF, YOU MUST FIRST SEND THOMPSON ABOARD.

HE WILL DELIVER THE MESSAGE THAT MAQUINNA MUST NOT BE HARMED.

AFTER THIS, SEVERAL MEN AND I WILL APPROACH THE SHIP TO PROPOSE AN EXCHANGE OF MAQUINNA FOR ME.

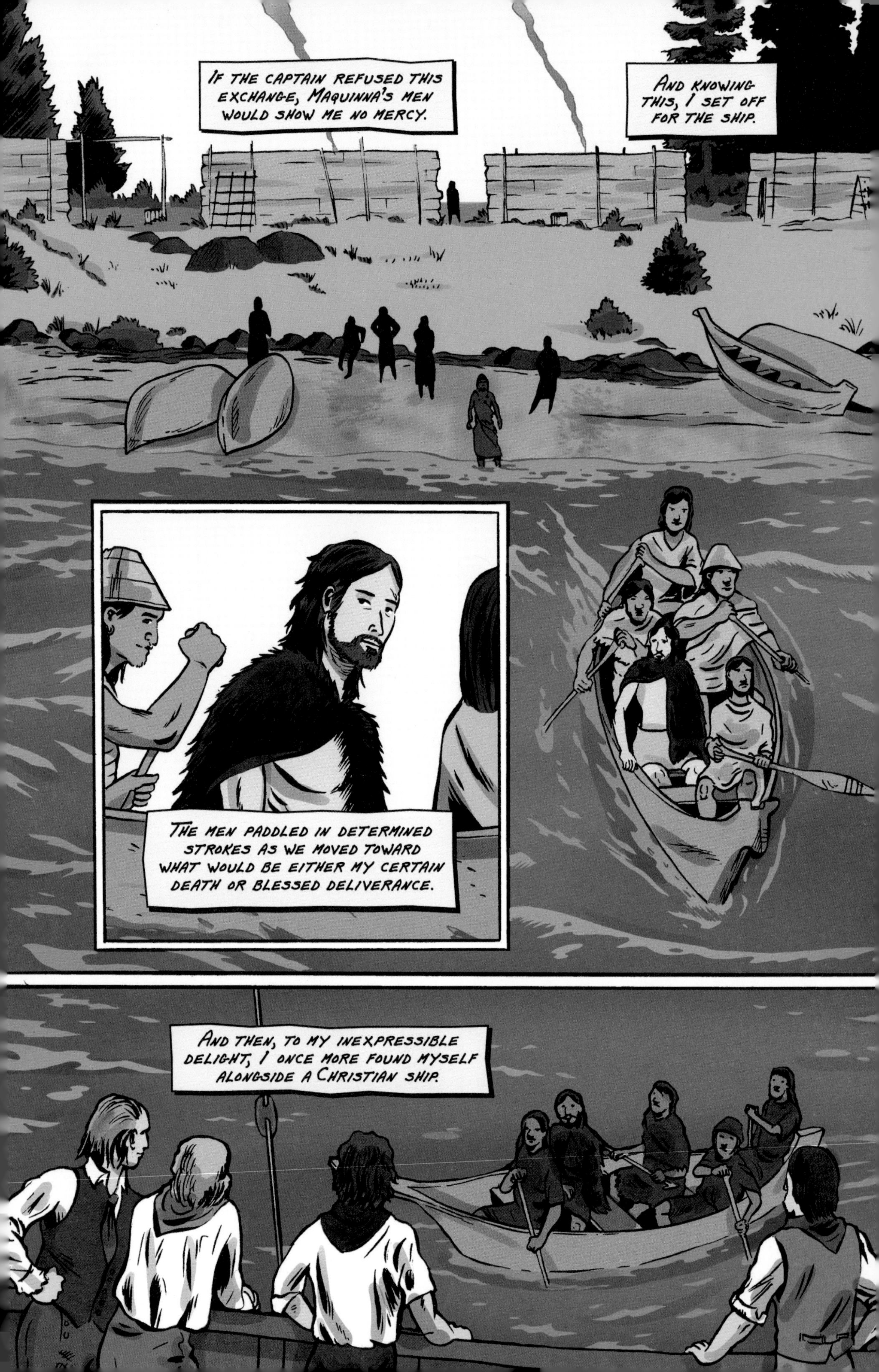
If the captain refused this exchange, Maquinna's men would show me no mercy.
And knowing this, I set off for the ship.
The men paddled in determined strokes as we moved toward what would be either my certain death or blessed deliverance.
And then, to my inexpressible delight, I once more found myself alongside a Christian ship.

SHE WAS CALLED THE *LYDIA* AND MY FELLOW CAPTIVE WAS THERE TO GREET ME.

WELL DONE, YOUNG MAN.

I AM CAPTAIN HILL.

I BELIEVE YOU KNOW THE PRISONER.

WOCASH, JOHN!

CAPTAIN, MAY I UNDO HIS IRONS?

*I GAVE MY ASSURANCE MAQUINNA POSED NO DANGER.*

INDEED, I FELT A SINCERE PLEASURE IN FREEING FROM SHACKLES A MAN WHO, THOUGH HE HAD CAUSED THE DEATH OF MY POOR COMRADES, HAD NEVERTHELESS PROVED TO BE MY FRIEND AND PROTECTOR.

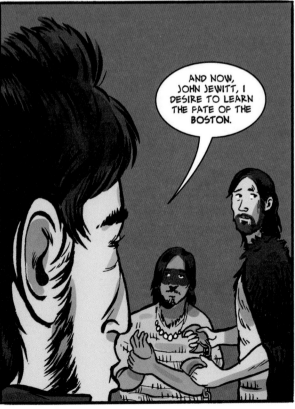

AND NOW, JOHN JEWITT, I DESIRE TO LEARN THE FATE OF THE BOSTON.

THIS MAN OUGHT TO BE KILLED! AND THE REST OF HIS MEN, TOO!

As he heard the tale, Captain Hill grew more and more irate.

I COULD LEVEL THEIR ENTIRE VILLAGE WITH MY CANNON!

AH, NO, GOOD SIR, YOU MUST UNDERSTAND...

I EXPLAINED THAT MAQUINNA HAD BEEN GRAVELY INSULTED BY CAPTAIN SALTER, AND THAT HIS PEOPLE HAD BEEN ABUSED AND EVEN KILLED WITH LITTLE PROVOCATION BY EARLIER CAPTAINS...

REVENGE IS A SACRED HONOR HERE.

KILLING THIS CHIEF WOULD SURELY LEAD TO MORE RETALIATION.

AND I COULD NEVER ALLOW THE DEATH OF A MAN WHO PRESERVED BOTH THOMPSON'S AND MY OWN LIFE!

I LEAVE THE FATE OF THIS MAN AND HIS PEOPLE IN YOUR HANDS, THEN.

KILL THEM OR NOT, AS YOU WILL!

LATER, WHEN WE WERE FINALLY ALONE, I TRIED TO REASSURE MAQUINNA.

CAPTAIN HILL WANTS ME DEAD.

I WILL CONVINCE HIM TO SPARE YOU...

...BUT YOU MUST RETURN WHAT LITTLE REMAINS OF THE BOSTON'S PROPERTY.

AND TAMSIN, HE MUST WANT ME DEAD AS WELL.

VERY PROBABLY. BUT I SHALL NOT ALLOW IT.

YOU MUST REMEMBER I PROTECTED YOU BOTH WHEN YOU HAD 500 ENEMIES.

YOU SHOULD DO THE SAME FOR ME NOW!

ALL WILL BE WELL TOMORROW. YOU WILL SEE.

THE NEXT MORNING, TOOWINNAKINNISH OFFERED MUCH OF WHAT WAS LEFT OF THE *BOSTON'S* BOOTY AND WAS MOST ANXIOUS TO COMFORT HIS CHIEF.

CAPTAIN HILL INSPECTED THE GOODS, INCLUDING SOME ARMS.

CHICK

HE DID NOT KNOW THAT ONE WAS LOADED WITH SWAN SHOT.

SNAP

BANG!

NHHG!

OH, MY FRIEND, WE ARE MUCH GRIEVED. THIS WAS NOT INTENTIONALLY DONE!

I KNOW MY FRIEND JOHN WOULD NEVER WISH ME HARM.

He bore the pain with great calmness and bade me farewell.

Toowinnakinnish had no part in the massacre of our crew and had always treated me with the greatest of hospitality and kindness.

To each of us, his death was a source of much affliction.

At daybreak, Maquinna's men returned the last of the *Boston's* cargo.

THE CAPTAIN SAYS HE WILL RETURN FOR TRADE IN NOVEMBER. I WILL SAVE MY BEST SKINS FOR YOU. PLEASE BRING MANY BLANKETS.

AND BISCUITS AND MOLASSES FOR SAT-SAT, WHO LOVES YOU SO WELL.

AS I DO.

ALTHOUGH I WILL NEVER ASK YOU TO WRITE ANOTHER LETTER FOR ME!

NOTWITHSTANDING MY JOY AT MY RESCUE...

...I STILL FELT A PAINFUL SENSATION AT PARTING WITH THIS CHIEF.

HE HAD PRESERVED MY LIFE AND GENERALLY SHOWED ME KINDNESS — MUCH BETTER TREATMENT THAN I COULD HAVE EXPECTED.

AND MY PLEASURE WAS MUCH DAMPED AT THE THOUGHT OF THE DEATH OF MY FRIEND TOOWINNAKINNISH. OF NOT SEEING SAT-SAT ANYMORE. OF MY YOUNG BRIDE OF SO FEW DAYS. OF A SOON-TO-BE-BORN CHILD I WOULD NEVER KNOW.

I DID NOT ALLOW HARM TO COME TO FRIENDLY COVE THAT DAY. INDEED, I LEFT A PART OF MYSELF BEHIND ON THAT WILD SHORE AS WE TURNED AWAY FROM NOOTKA, TOWARD MY FREEDOM... AND FINALLY HOME.

JOHN JEWITT FINALLY SETTLED IN NEW
ENGLAND IN 1807, AND IMMEDIATELY
PUBLISHED HIS JOURNALS FROM NOOTKA.
AN EXPANDED VERSION, KNOWN AS THE
"NARRATIVE," APPEARED IN 1815 AND A
THEATRICAL STAGING FOLLOWED SOON AFTER.

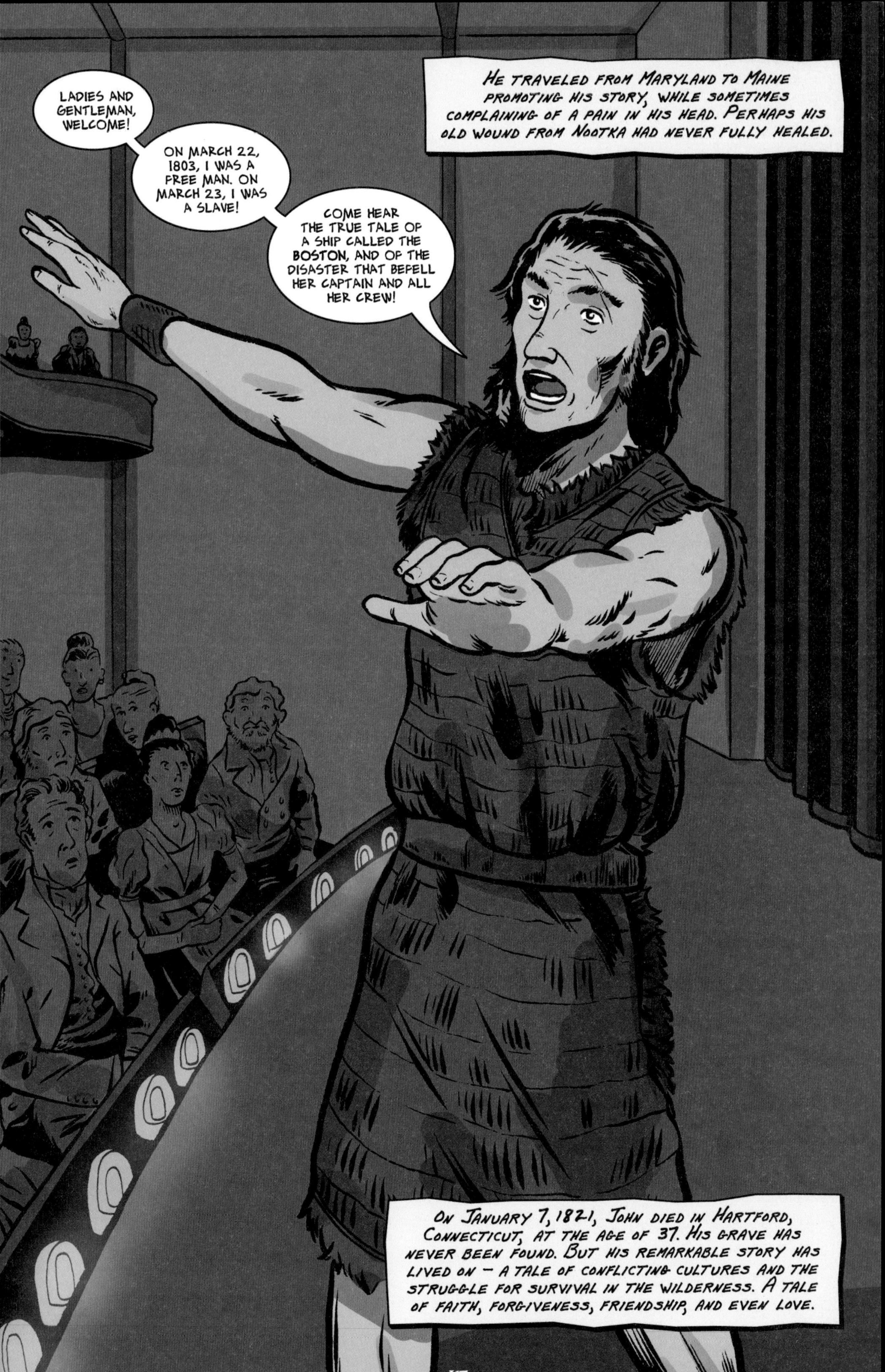
HE TRAVELED FROM MARYLAND TO MAINE PROMOTING HIS STORY, WHILE SOMETIMES COMPLAINING OF A PAIN IN HIS HEAD. PERHAPS HIS OLD WOUND FROM NOOTKA HAD NEVER FULLY HEALED.
LADIES AND GENTLEMAN, WELCOME!
ON MARCH 22, 1803, I WAS A FREE MAN. ON MARCH 23, I WAS A SLAVE!
COME HEAR THE TRUE TALE OF A SHIP CALLED THE BOSTON, AND OF THE DISASTER THAT BEFELL HER CAPTAIN AND ALL HER CREW!
ON JANUARY 7, 1821, JOHN DIED IN HARTFORD, CONNECTICUT, AT THE AGE OF 37. HIS GRAVE HAS NEVER BEEN FOUND. BUT HIS REMARKABLE STORY HAS LIVED ON – A TALE OF CONFLICTING CULTURES AND THE STRUGGLE FOR SURVIVAL IN THE WILDERNESS. A TALE OF FAITH, FORGIVENESS, FRIENDSHIP, AND EVEN LOVE.

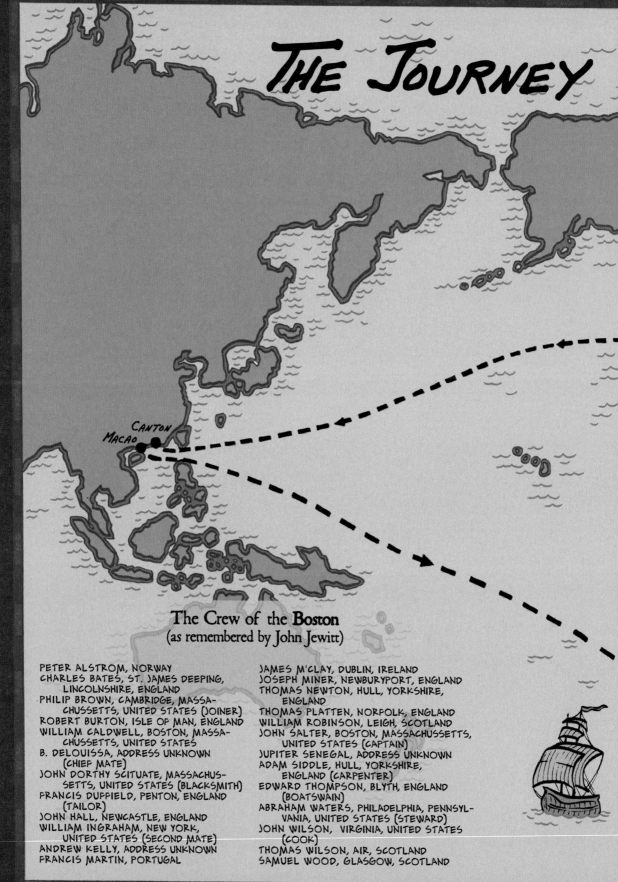

# THE JOURNEY

CANTON
MACAO

## The Crew of the Boston
### (as remembered by John Jewitt)

PETER ALSTROM, NORWAY
CHARLES BATES, ST. JAMES DEEPING,
    LINCOLNSHIRE, ENGLAND
PHILIP BROWN, CAMBRIDGE, MASSA-
    CHUSSETTS, UNITED STATES (JOINER)
ROBERT BURTON, ISLE OF MAN, ENGLAND
WILLIAM CALDWELL, BOSTON, MASSA-
    CHUSSETTS, UNITED STATES
B. DELOUISSA, ADDRESS UNKNOWN
    (CHIEF MATE)
JOHN DORTHY SCITUATE, MASSACHUS-
    SETTS, UNITED STATES (BLACKSMITH)
FRANCIS DUFFIELD, PENTON, ENGLAND
    (TAILOR)
JOHN HALL, NEWCASTLE, ENGLAND
WILLIAM INGRAHAM, NEW YORK,
    UNITED STATES (SECOND MATE)
ANDREW KELLY, ADDRESS UNKNOWN
FRANCIS MARTIN, PORTUGAL

JAMES M'CLAY, DUBLIN, IRELAND
JOSEPH MINER, NEWBURYPORT, ENGLAND
THOMAS NEWTON, HULL, YORKSHIRE,
    ENGLAND
THOMAS PLATTEN, NORFOLK, ENGLAND
WILLIAM ROBINSON, LEIGH, SCOTLAND
JOHN SALTER, BOSTON, MASSACHUSSETTS,
    UNITED STATES (CAPTAIN)
JUPITER SENEGAL, ADDRESS UNKNOWN
ADAM SIDDLE, HULL, YORKSHIRE,
    ENGLAND (CARPENTER)
EDWARD THOMPSON, BLYTH, ENGLAND
    (BOATSWAIN)
ABRAHAM WATERS, PHILADELPHIA, PENNSYL-
    VANIA, UNITED STATES (STEWARD)
JOHN WILSON, VIRGINIA, UNITED STATES
    (COOK)
THOMAS WILSON, AIR, SCOTLAND
SAMUEL WOOD, GLASGOW, SCOTLAND

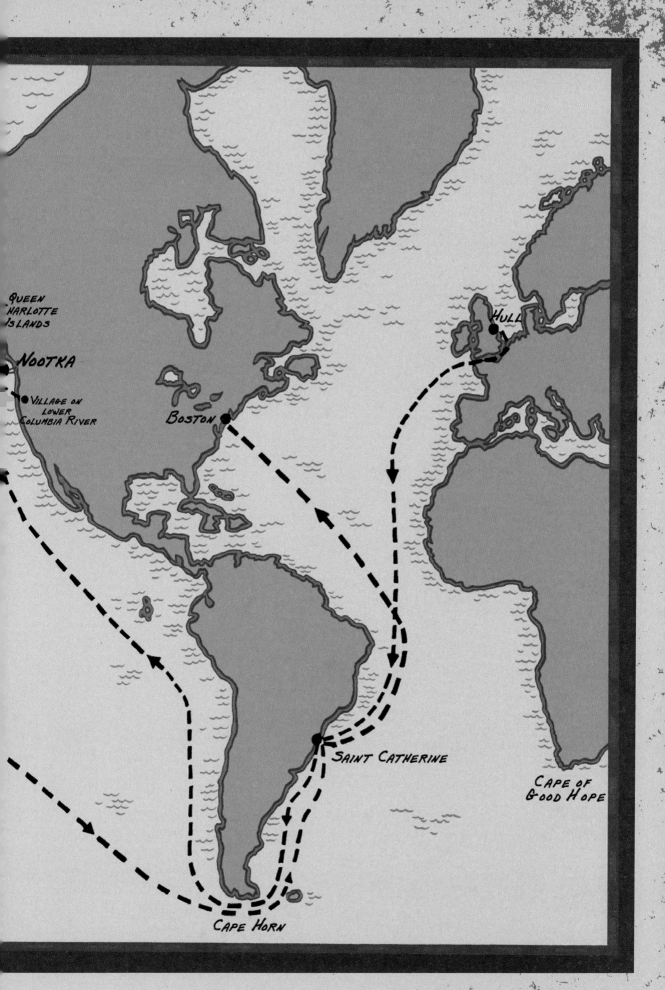

QUEEN
CHARLOTTE
ISLANDS

NOOTKA

Village on
Lower
Columbia River

BOSTON

HULL

SAINT CATHERINE

CAPE OF
GOOD HOPE

CAPE HORN

# A List of Commonly Spoken Words in the Nootkan Language
### (phonetic pronunciations compiled by John Jewitt)

## Common Nouns

| | |
|---|---|
| Bear | Moo-watch |
| Brother | Katlahtik |
| Canoe | Chap-atz |
| Child | Tanassis |
| Cloth | Toop-helth |
| Cod | Toosch-qua |
| Copper | Chee-pokes |
| Daughter | Tanassis-kloots-mah |
| Ears | Parpee |
| Earth | Klat-tur-miss |
| Eyes | Kassee |
| Father | Noowexa |
| Feet | Klish-klin |
| Fire / fuel | Een-nuk-see |
| Fishhook | Chee-me-na |
| Fishhooks | Chee-men |
| Fruit | Cham-mass |
| Goose / duck | Mar-met-ta |
| Hair | Hap-se-up |
| Halibut | Pow-ee |
| Hands | Kook-a-nik-sa |
| Head | Tau-hat-se-tee |
| Herring | Kloos-a-mit |
| House | Muk-ka-tee |
| Iron | Sick-a-minny |
| Knife / dagger | Chit-ta-yek |
| Man | Check-up |
| Mother | Hooma-hexa |
| Mountain / hill | Noot-chee |
| No | Wik |
| Nose | Naetsa |
| Oil | Klack-e-miss |
| Paddle | Oo-wha-pa |
| Powder | Moot-sus |
| Rain | Meetla |
| Rings | Klick-er-yek |
| Rock | Mook-see |
| Salmon | So-har |
| Sea | Toop-elth |
| Seal | Coo-coo-ho-sa |
| Sea otter | Quart-lak |
| Sister | Kloot-chem-up |
| Sky | Sie-yah |
| Slave | Kak-koelth |
| Smoke | Quish-ar |
| Snow | Queece |
| Son | Tanassis-check-up |
| Stars | Tar-toose |
| Sun / Moon | Oophelth |
| Sweet | Cham-mass-ish |
| Teeth | Chee-chee |
| Tongue | Choop |
| Warrior | Ar-smootish-check-up |
| Water (fresh) | Cha-hak |
| Whale | Mah-hack |
| Woman | Klootz-mah |
| Yes | He-ho |

## Common Adjectives

| | |
|---|---|
| Enough | Nee-sim-mer-hise |
| Hungry | Hah-welks |
| Much | I-yah-ish |

## Common Verbs

| | |
|---|---|
| To bathe | Ar-teese |
| To blow | Pook-shit-tle |
| To kindle a fire | Een-a-qui-shit-tle |
| To go fish | Ma-mook-su-mah |
| To laugh | Kle-whar |
| To play | Em-me-chap |
| To sell | Ma-kook |

## Numbers

| | |
|---|---|
| One | Sah-wauk |
| Two | Att-la |
| Three | Kat-sa |
| Four | Mooh |
| Five | Soo-chah |
| Six | Noo-poo |
| Seven | At-tle-poo |
| Eight | At-lah-quelth |
| Nine | Saw-wauk-quelth |
| Ten | Hy-o |
| Twenty | Sak-aitz |
| One hundred | Soo-jewk |
| One thousand | Hy-e-oak |

# Acknowledgments

Among the many people who helped bring this project to fruition, I must first thank
John Jewitt the 6th and Mike Maquinna the 8th, both of whom were kind enough
to share insights about their ancestors, the John and Maquinna characters who are
featured in this book. I am grateful to all the Mowachaht/Muchalaht First Nations
people who welcomed us so warmly to Yuquot, most especially Eugene Amos, a gentle
spirit, despite the scary tattoos.

My most sincere gratitude goes to three wonderfully gifted and generous artists—
Mike Short, Matt Dembicki, and Evan Keeling—who penciled, inked, and colored way
into the wee hours.

Richard Inglis provided scores of visual references, fielded hundreds of questions, and
caught a thousand errors, for which I owe him a million thanks.

Robert Kraft recorded interviews; snapped photos; ushered me through the Strathcona
Forest and up the Muchalat Inlet to Nootka Sound, and finally to Yuquot itself; read
countless drafts; and provided unflagging enthusiasm for this book, from inception to
its conclusion.

Dr. Cole Harris, Professor Emeritus, Dept. of Geographical History, University of British
Columbia; Dane Bevan, of the Oregon Historical Society; and Martha Black of the
Royal British Columbia Museum all took the time to share their perspectives on the
story. Naturalist Birgit Buhleier helped me distinguish a "right whale" from a wrong
one, and Joe Follansbee of Grays Harbor Historical Seaport Authority helped me sort
out a sloop from a brig.

Micah Farritor, John Kovalesky, and Sergio Ragno all provided invaluable artistic assis-
tance.

The team at Fulcrum: Sam Scinta, Rebecca McEwen, Melanie Roth, Jessica Townsend
were steadfast supporters throughout the process. Thanks also to Fred Chao, Alison
Auch, Haley Berry, Elaine English, and Sally Crane.

And finally, my thanks to John Rodgers Jewitt, 1783–1821.

**Rebecca Goldfield** is an award-winning writer/producer of documentary films, with a focus on history and science. Her work has aired on National Public Radio (NPR), PBS, The Discovery Channel, and National Geographic TV among others. She was also a contributor to the Harvey-nominated graphic novel, *District Comics*, and is presently developing several graphic novels based on great true stories. Goldfield splits her time between Washington D.C., rural Pennsylvania, and New York City, but still spends a much time as she can in Vancouver, B.C.

**Mike Short** lives and works in Lorton, Virginia, and spends his free time watching movies with his wife Danette, playing with his kids, chasing his runaway dogs, or burning the midnight oil drawing comics with friends. He was a contributor to the Eisner-nominated and Aesop Prize winning *Trickster*, and his comics frequently appear in *Magic Bullet*, a free comics newspaper published by the DC Conspiracy. You can connect with him on Twitter at @mikeyboy42, and on Tumblr at mikeysketches.tumblr.com.

**Matt Dembicki** previously edited and contributed to the Eisner-nominated and Aesop Prize winning *Trickster: Native American Tales: A Graphic Collection*. He also served at the helm of *Wild Ocean: Sharks, Whales, Rays, and Other Endangered Sea Creatures*, and *District Comics: An Unconventional History of Washington, D.C.*, a Harvey Award nominated anthology that was named as one of the best books of 2012 by the *Washington Post*.

**Evan Keeling** is a founding member of the DC Conspiracy, a comic creator collective founded ten years ago in Washington, D.C. He has worked on comic projects including *Crumbsnatchers, Codename: Fifinella, Xoc: Journey of a Great White*, and the Eisner-nominated and Aesop Prize winning *Trickster*. He is currently working on a series of comics about the D.C. punk scene in the '90s called *DC Punk*. Evan Keeling lives in Washington, D.C.., with his wife and daughter. You can find out more about him at his website, www.etkeeling.com.